Touching the Pastor's Wife

D.L. PEAVY

ISBN: 978-0-578-43311-0

i

Read responsibly

ACKNOWLEDGMENTS

So, here we are. At the end of our first Novel. I say we, because I value all of you who were involved with this project. This section of the book is definitely the hardest for me to conclude because there are so many people who have made me a better writer, a more creative writer, yet my gratitude on paper would do no justice in explaining how deeply grateful I am. First, I must say, I serve a God who can change any situation, no matter what it looks like. Erica Peavy, you are truly a blessing in my life, thank you for sacrificing sleep, time, and your own personal goals to help create my vision. Thank you for believing in me and never allowing me to give up on anything. Thank you for reading over my manuscript repeatedly until I got it right. You are truly my best friend. Rhonda Sue Calhoun, (Mama) you took me to my first open mic, where I fell in love with the art of spoken word and literature, I've been writing ever since. You've always encouraged me beyond the possibilities. If ever I lose hope, I'll remember the mother that worked two and sometimes three jobs just to create hope. To my family Randy Calhoun, Lawanda Terry, Kirktrece Mims, extended family, in-laws, and close friends, I love you forever and always will! Rachel Barbee, Riviera Paris, Ja'keva Lavely,

Tiffany Lewis, and Tamela Newman, thank you ladies for being the biggest advocates for my first book. To my illustrator, Money Graphics, you are the best. Darren Coby, you are simply dope! Thank you for listening to all my crazy ideas, for taking time from your family to record and shoot scenes, you've contributed so much into the promotion of this project. You are my brother and a man of many talents; I believe you are destined to be great and I'm forever grateful for you. Branden Cartwright, what can I say... there are no true words to describe our brotherhood. From the moment you said to me, – *"Let God be true."*— I knew you were the truth. Reminiscing and creating business plans with you will never get old. Thank you for always being positive energy. Sidney Webster, thank you so much for all your hard work during this process, thank you for always being available at a moment's notice. I admire the God-fearing woman you are, and I appreciate the numerous pep talks of encouragement. Special thanks to my readers. Thank you for allowing me to share my creative side with you. I hope that you enjoy this book and future books to come.

Yours truly,

D.L Peavy.

Touching the Pastor's Wife

D.L. PEAVY

DERRICK

In the Beginning

I was fully committed to a daze, daydreaming in a world of my own during the "joy of gospel" as they called it. Have you ever had stupid thoughts or visions in an inappropriate place?

SHUT THE FUCK UP! …is what I tried to tell the part of my corrupt brain that controlled my careless ass cogitation system, which clearly has no filter. To be honest, it's crazy that I imagined our tall, innocent, dark and thick bodied Pastor, standing over my wife, naked with sweat dripping from his short cut head of hair. It was as if they had been fucking for hours. His dick was propped deep in her mouth. As he edged toward her throat, her puffy, pale, dimpled cheeks filled with saliva. She was persistent and trying to fit more in, gripping his manly monster, forcing it forward. His large hands palmed the back of her head while running his oversized fingers through her smooth copper hair, and as usual, her ass was poking out like a black woman. She was submissive like a porn-star on her knees, confirming his will with extra saliva lingering from his

hard-vainglorious pride of fruit, his toes started to curl. Just as she gagged and right before I got even more disturbed, I heard a pound from the drums bringing me back in tune with reality.

"Temptation will lead you to hell. Therefore, be cautious of your actions!"

Pastor Herman repeated.

"Be cautious of your actions! This means that you should not allow sinful trouble to perform where God is working. Amen?"

Following the pastor's lead, the church agreeing said amen in unity, I felt the guilt within like he was speaking directly to me. It was as if he knew about the recent affairs I had with certain members of the church, or maybe he saw me staring at sister Stacy's fine apple-shaped ass from behind while my wife was turned the other way. I'm yet to confess my slight addiction for beautiful ageless women to anyone, instead I pretended to be eagerly involved holding Amber's hand tightly, convinced that I loved her more than anything. Maybe I'm forcing myself to be convinced in the light, know that the darkness carry's the truth of my sinful color's, but those doors remain shut.

The church gradually went into a deep spiritual cleanse. Random outburst of "Glory to God!" and "Hallelujah!" filled the atmosphere over A gospel melody played softly by the drums and piano simultaneously. Some of the church folk seem accessibly effected like he pinched a nerve with his choice of words. A lot of them started expressing noticeable emotions with tears and body language including my wife Amber. She stood in silence with both of her hands held high in the same position as that kid who got killed by the police a few weeks ago.

Looking at the entire scene made me nervous. After a while I got close to nodding off then Pastor interrupted with his loud ass mouth.

SOMEWHERE BETWEEN TEMPTATION AND PROVERBS 21

"The only way to cleanse your spirit is to open your heart, there is nothing bigger than GOD, don't worry about the battle, just embrace it, because it's not happening to you, it's happening for you. Seed without rain won't harvest! Your storm has purpose it's not by mistake nor mishap, it's designed specifically for you, amen respect the process. Scripture alone supports the idea that we should fall back and allow God to work, he doesn't need help, remember it was his grace!" said Pastor Herman.

He left that grace word to linger as members quickly took notice, encouraging him to continue.

"Yes Sir, come on now…"

"Preach Pastor!"

He walked up to one of the deacons placing his left

hand on his shoulder, they looked into each other's eyes as if they shared a bromance with a level of trust and understanding. And in a distinct high-pitch, that was borderline cry-ish like, he went on…

"…Your past doesn't get to dictate who the holy Father is creating you to be. The power of God is among us, make this your own personal prayer, right here right now draw in, don't wait until tomorrow fore it may never come."

He held the microphone by his waistline pacing back and forth across the stage praying to himself. He was fully engaged in the moment along with the members of the church. Some days I want to give in to this life of discipline but can't help feeling like the only sinner in the room who God isn't fucking with and today was no different. I didn't feel one spirit, and nobody's holy ghost touched me, unless the spirit was a freak creating my inconvenience, because my ego was solid. All eight-inch seven quarter round was poking through my jeans, likely from a combination of the mild chill in the room and this thick booty chick directly in front of me. She was slaying this tightly fitted, flower pattern dress. If God is real, I definitely deserve a pass seeing how I don't control the thermostat and the attire this bitch has on is borderline inappropriate for church. She knows what the hell she's doing though, my mouth got extra damp, to the point it was beyond me, I've never wanted to eat ass so bad in my life. I was low-key gazing hard as fuck, trying to imagine her face down with my hands separating those Georgia ass cheeks, exposing that pretty brown peach. On my Uncle Paul, rest his soul, my tongue wouldn't hesitate to apply a natural K-Y with permission. Her ass was drawing a nigga in. Every time she jumped for glory that mug jiggled something decent, which is far past overwhelming for a man of my magnitude.

I held the church program over my private area to prevent my bold bulge from being exposed. The musicians played seamlessly like they've done a thousand times. Pastor Herman raised the microphone up to speak after several minutes of the hole church meditating.

"Come on! This is our worship prayer."

He turned to the drummer signaling for him to fade out leaving the piano to produce a smooth pleasing quality of sound, setting the tone to deliver his closing message. In a sarcastic church like laugh connected with a stutter he continued…

"Ha ha s-s--see you can chase and acquire all things and never find God! But if you trust in him enough to keep your worrisome behind still and watch him move in your life, you can acquire him with ease. (Psalms 46:10) simply says "Be still for I am God" –*"Aw man that's good,"*-- if you want to be close to God, be still! You don't have to chase after something he wants you to have, when you inherit him from your faithfulness, blessings will manifest and develop in your favor, because he is an all-purpose God. But let's be honest, some of us so bougie we only like hearing the good about our cute little problem, verses having a simple conversation with God, who's going to give us the sloppy truth about our ugly mess. ("Yes Pastor that's good") Who am I talking to this morning? We would rather hide behind a pretty mental storefront than allow God to show us how messy it is in the back room. But if I can be direct, and here it is, having an honest conversation with God is easier than any text you can ever send to an unstable source that will ultimately fail you. Open your heart and your mouth! You can be a silent foolish texting foo if you want to, but I know his worth, see some of y'all still quite like you don't need his mercy, like you got it all figured out. At minimum you should be screaming at the top of your lungs that he thought your raggedy tail was worth saving!" ("Amen hallelujah!")

Pastor stood up there looking super emotional like he really believed in the message he was providing to these people.

"Jesus is the center", is all I recall before hearing the music raise along with collection buckets that begin to float in rotation, I watched on judgingly as these fools gave a large portion of what I assume was the last of what they had left to make it through the week, in exchange for plan B prayer. Meanwhile I was cheating their system by putting some change in my envelope without filling it out, Amber looked at me crazy.

"Really?" What? I didn't put our names on it."

"Childish very childish…" she half-way joked.

She crossed her legs and turned away, I plead my case in a whispering tone. She called me stupid and continued to play me off. The music faded and Pastor Herman passed the microphone to first lady Victoria's fine, light-skinned ass. She walked like she was hiding some good pussy between them legs, smiling at her husband with a glow during the exchange. I whispered in Amber's ear again, "Thank God, I'm just about churched out for the year after all that damn preaching.

I'm sure I missed some good football highlights." ...

"Shhh, pay attention." she hissed, tapping my leg.

First Lady went into her regular closing routine.

A Sinner's Truth

After it was all said and done most of the prayer seekers flooded the altar, Amber whispered, "Derrick" followed by a motionless pull, I released her hand effortlessly and watched as she made her way to the altar alone with disappointment on her face. In my head I thought to myself *I'm not ready for this place...* But my heart feels different at times. Aside from my personal feelings, our daughter Ashley is wakened by the chaos that came with the noisy dismissal,

"Daddy..." She said lazily.

I comforted my baby girl, cradling her in my arms ready to go to the car. We moved slowly through the crowd inching our way to the main entrance. I was reluctant to participate in any conversations, mainly to avoid all the seductive ass around me. Unfortunately, my hazel eyes couldn't help but to wonder curiously with excitement. I was literally three feet from the door before seeing a familiar face that gave me what I thought was a significant reason to give in to my flirtatious ways. "Oh hey, what's good Kim?" Having flashbacks about how fast she made me cum three weeks ago with that wide damn tongue finessing the area between my ass and balls, she's a different type of nasty, but I happen to I like it. I gave my phone to Ashley to keep her occupied before looking around to make sure Amber was nowhere in sight. I got as close as possible, with Ashley in arm, then whispered "When are you free?" Followed by my tongue rolling off her earlobe. She squirmed before biting her bottom lip.

"How about tonight?"

I gave a slight seductive look that suggested a strong possibility, then hit her with words of uncertainty.

"Aw yeah, we'll see, but you know firsthand a married man can't guarantee."

"I also know that a married man won't turn it down if it's free. Plus, I know she not swallowing them babies like me, don't keep me waiting."

Almost forgetting we were in a public setting, we left

it at that, and parted ways Ashley and I headed out the door spotting Marcel in the parking lot. I tried my best not to be seen by the stocky 6'5 gentle giant, as we approached, but he never fails to notice and acknowledge me.

He spoke in a generous tone. "Hey Princess, look at you, you're getting big girly, how old are you now, twenty? Can I use your phone?" she laughed.

He reached out and gave her a soft two finger tickle, Ashley being her shy self, smiled then cuddled her face into my shoulder.

"What's going on brother Derrick, it's been a couple of Sundays everything okay? You been good?"

"Most definitely, just been busy here lately," I replied.

"Yeah life will do that, I see you know how to keep lil mama busy too, this technology is something else, all in a cell phone, can you believe it?"

"Aw man, if that's not a true statement I don't know what is. I'll never understand kids watching other kids play with toys on the internet, that would have never been our generation."

"Right, sticks, rocks, and tag outside was all that we had maybe even a milkcrate for basketball if we were lucky and there was no running in and out, these millennium kids have it made. How's life been treating you though?"

"Good man just working and living life. Same ole same, you know how that goes. How about yourself?" I asked, regretting the question the second I asked, like I really gave a damn. I made as little eye contact as possible. staring at his bright orange vest for most of our engagement.

"Yea, I hear you brother, I have to work tonight myself."

Little did he know; I knew his schedule better than he did. I pretended to be somewhat interested in his mediocre conversation.

"Hey if you don't work you don't eat right?" … I said.

Like clockwork, I waited for him to quote scripture.

"Well you know Colossians 3:23 speaks to my heart, 'What he does, do it heartily as to the Lord, and not unto men.' I live my life as if God is watching." he shared confidently.

Yes sir, is generally all I can ever say after people give me some holy talk like I really knew anything about the bible, let alone scripture or the God that no one has ever seen, that they speak so highly of.

"Well brother Marcel I'll see you this Tuesday or

maybe next Sunday. This little girl of mine is getting heavy. We shared a fake laugh before going our separate ways.

"Okay see you both soon, take care and God bless"

"Yes Sir."

I made it to the car as soon as my arm went numb. I sat Ashley in her booster seat.

"Where is Mommy?"

"On her way baby. Hey how about we eat ice cream for dinner?"

"Oouu! Yes, Daddy please."

"I'm kidding love bug we can't do that."

"Aww why not?"

"Because all our teeth would fall out honey."

She put her head down, sad about my response.

"Aww not fair."

"Yea I know boo boo, but hey Tuesday we can go get some ice cream while mommy is at work, how does that sound?"

"Okay Daddy."

Her spirits lifted some. We waited a short while before Amber arrived slamming the door with force.

"Is that necessary?" I asked.

Reasoning with myself thinking she couldn't have

seen my encounter with Kim, but her mystery crime solving ass is sneaky. Even still, I had to hope that she didn't.

"What's your problem now Amber!?"

Still not a word just awkward silence as we drove off. Even Ashley wasn't being her normal talkative self, which is odd for a 5-year old.

Halfway through our ride home, the silence breaks in an unpleasant tone.

"Why don't you ever fasten up her seat belt Derrick?"

"Excuse me. I forgot; people forget stuff Amber it's no big deal. Everybody can't be perfect like you, so stop acting like it's a long ass ride. She'll be alright."

I reached my right hand back to Ashley, she stretched her short arm to place her small hand in mine, something we usually do on our rides together.

Amber began rubbing her hand against her face and scratching her head. I could tell she was ready to snap.

"That's not the point Derrick! You're so fucking careless with everything, including me! Sometimes I feel like I'm the only one who's trying. It's like you're here physically, but nowhere to be found emotionally. I thought I married a man Derrick!"

"Whoa, wait. Hold the fuck up!" I replied in my

deepest voice.

"I am a man dammit! Oh, I get it... you think just because you bring home more money than me, I'm not a man huh? You want me to be one of them white collar muthafuckers huh?"

"Money?! No one said anything about money Derrick! That has nothing to do with what I am talking about and you know it! Stop being so ignorant, you made the choice not to finish getting your degree for whatever reason. Hell, only you know."

"I made the best decision for our family at that time."

"I wish you would stop using your challenges in life to downplay me, I do what's best for us as well, so if I have an opportunity to better myself along with the life of my family which includes your dumbass, that's what I'll do and continue to do. I support your black ass in every decision you make, for once I wish you would support me."

"Well what are you saying huh? What the fuck does that mean? I'm not a man, you want a white boy?"

"I never said anything about wanting someone else. You're so clueless, you know what never mind Derrick, nothing at all just forget it!"

With frustration in her face she continued to be blunt

in her outpour.

"You know sometimes I just want to give up, but I keep my faith in God and pray. That's all I can do I guess."

She took a deep breath; time was the cure that brought peace to her nerves allowing her to speak to me calmly.

"Oh yeah by the way I saw --"

Suspiciously I interrupted.

"You saw what?"

She looked at me strangely before finishing her sentence with an attitude.

"I was just going to tell you that I saw Deacon Mike talking to Pastor and First Lady, they all asked me to say hello to you."

Feeling like an idiot I relaxed some.

"What else did they say?"

It was apparent that she was irritated by my presence.

"That's all Derrick! What were they supposed to say? Hell, you never come to speak making me look and feel stupid all the time." Knowing I had skeletons to hide I decided not to piss her off any further. By now we shared a mutual attitude like it was her time of the month. I pulled into the driveway and swiftly shifted the gear in park then tossed the keys in her lap. From the back-seat Ashley stared out the window watching our neighbor's kids jump fearlessly on their trampoline. Impatiently she repeated.

"I want to play! Can I play?"

I opened the door grabbing her from the back, allowing her to join in on the action.

"Now I guess you expect me to sit here and watch her huh, soon as she falls or hurts herself just know you're going to be the one up all night at the emergency room."

"Why do you always go to the extreme Amber? Damn Virgo's man I swear y'all extra, why would you even speak that negative shit in the universe? Knock on some wood, goodness gracious! She will be fine, let the girl live geesshh. And it's not like you were coming in anyway. We both know how this works. You get an attitude, cut me off, until you realize it's not that deep because it's never that deep. Is it?" She sat firm in anger watching Ashley play in the distance.

"Yea, okay whatever."

I made my way into the house, finding peace in my normal spot. My anything-goes-while-Amber-is-asleep spot -- the guestroom.

I rest my head on a loose pillow, folding it in half before replying to text messages I received from women whose real names I may have never really known. Most of them I named in code according to the places where I met them. Like one of Ashley's daycare teachers who's contact name is registered in my phone under "The homie Dc". I scrolled through the messages finding them to be short and boring. Just some "Hellos" and "Good mornings" not nearly enough to keep me entertained or awake.

I felt super drained from waking up early this morning to please Amber's church fetish. I took advantage of the me time in the guestroom, grabbing my abortion towel from between the mattress. I begin to do what I knew best, please the inner me with some mature self-love.

I closed my eyes to fantasize about one of the multiple women I smashed whose sex was dope enough for me to remember. I can only imagine how Amber would react, along with the shit she would talk if she knew first-hand how excited I got about stroking myself to different women. I took extra precaution making sure the door was locked before getting careless. I closed my eyes to link with the sensation that my wife has rarely provided here lately, wrapping my dominant hand right below the head of my flexible snake squeezing it back and forth with a violent twist that quickly had me about to release the return on my investment. I tried my best to hold my nut just to maintain the feeling a while longer but thinking about hitting Tosha's big head ass from behind while pulling her synthetic hair just enough to loosen them raggedy ass braids hiding underneath, did it every time.

I replayed our experiences to a tee, it had me feeling so good. I had to remind my brain to quiet my mouth after the first, "Ouu shit!" slipped out a bit louder than expected. Relaxation from relieving myself filled my body.

I laid motionless for a minute or two before gaining the energy to wipe up the warm slimy mess. I fixed myself back to normal and closed my eyes for what seemed like a brief moment before reopening them to darkness all around me. I was pleased to see new message notifications on my phone. I rubbed my eyes clear, only to discover that it was 12:23am and Kim had already sent three text messages.

"Your wife sleep yet?"

"Come get this pussy, I'm so wet"

"DERRICK GET UP!"

My heart raced with excitement. I quickly replied, **"I'll be there soon."** Almost immediately she responded.

"About time! We only have until 6 hurry up!"

After washing my dick off, I battled with myself not wanting to leave my home with tension in the air. I quietly creeped into our room to find Ashley asleep beside her mother. I carried her to her bed placing her in the center and pulling the cover to her shoulders. I brushed my fingers across her warm cheeks before heading back across the hall where Amber laid with her legs tangled under the sheets.

Looking at her from the foot of the bed. Headfirst, I made my way. Her body tossed a bit as I began sucking on her toes, working my way up to her thighs. Her light snore gradually faded. I moved her panties to the side and immediately put my lips on her warm passion fruit. I've never been a sloppy eater, but I felt like I owed her. I went all in trying to snatch her soul. Sliding my tongue in and out repeatedly, creating an overflow of her juicy arrangement. Her hands massaged the back of my head. Her moans got louder, giving me motivation to keep going. I extended my arm to caress one of her breasts. Aroused, she wrapped her thighs around my head like earmuffs. I felt my penis rising as she forced my face closer to her vagina rocking back and forth fucking the saliva out of my mouth. I fingered her at a pleasurable pace and continued sucking on her soft pearl. Her thighs got tight as she arched her back. She moaned,

"I'm about to cum, ooo Chris!" --- I instantly hopped the fuck up wiping her discharge from my chin.

"What the fuck! Who the fuck is Chris!"

"Huh?" She said in a dumb sounding voice.

"You heard me Amber! Don't play stupid now, who the hell is Chris!?"

"Shhh don't be so loud you're going to wake up your child."

"Don't shhh me. Who the fuck is Chris!?"

"I'm sorry Derrick. I was half sleep babe. You know that's my ex, the one who passed away, I was dreaming."

"OH, you were sleep huh…Yea whatever Amber! So, you're dreaming about fucking the deceased while I'm suffocating trying to get you right."

"I don't know what I was dreaming, I said I was sorry Derrick. I'm sure you think about other bitches all the time."

She was right but I would never admit that. I washed my face in the master bathroom replying

"Nope, just you!"

"Okay, sure Derrick." I grabbed her keys off her nightstand and told her I would be back.

"Why are you taking my car?"

"Because I don't feel like stopping to put gas in mine. Plus, you have me blocked in the garage remember smart ass. Dang, what's it matter to you anyway? What's yours is mine and what's mine is yours, right? Isn't that what you said earlier?"

"That only works when you have something to share foo" she joked.

"So, we on that again, you're really going there once again huh?" I said, missing the joke.

"Get out your feelings KeKe I was just playing with you dang, now look who can't take a joke."

"Just note that's the second time tonight that you called me someone else."

"Dude hush, the first time was an accident and I said sorry. If you can't see the humor in me calling you KeKe and telling you to get out of your feelings then maybe I need to buy a strap-on."

"Yea you must still be sleepy talking irresponsible like that and by the way, saying the word foo is a sin, Church woman."

"Whatever negro you're the one who's going to hell for not coming forward to let someone pray for you, knowing you need it -- knowing we need it."

"Well I'm glad we can laugh about it now with yo uptight ass."

"Oh, it's not going to be funny when you're in that fiery pit begging for mercy."

"You said you pray for me all the time, right? How many people do I need to pray for me? You act like I'm dying from cancer, and at the end of the day, if I go to hell, were going together."

"The hell we not!"

I laughed at her dumb ass on my way out the room door.

"Bring me some double fudge ice cream back and don't be at that strip club giving what little of the so-called money we do have away to them hoes you, Issac, and Jazz sneaky asses be

mingling with. You shouldn't be going to drink anyway when you know you have to drive home!"

"What? Nobody is mingling with anyone, and no one is drinking on a Sunday Amber."

"Well it's Monday now sweetheart and I don't need my car all wrecked up, some people never learn..." she mumbled under her breath. I retracted back to the doorway.

"It was one DUI and I wasn't even drunk he was just a bored racist cop."

"Sure Derrick, every white cop is raciest right?"

"Hey most of your people are racists Amber, you forget that part, your own mom was raciest before she knew me."

"No, my mother has never been racist she just didn't like you at first. To be racist is to stay racist." she said confidently.

"Man, whatever, shut your country sounding ass up she still doesn't like me."

"You shut your, yes a master roots sounding ass up"

"Aw yeah...What's that about? You know what I don't even want to know."

"Well you started it."

"Whatever white girl I'll be back."   .

"Yo mama"

"Hey, hey now watch it."

IT'S ONLY A CRIME
IF YOU GET CAUGHT

I turned out to the main road spraying on a dab of Gucci Guilty. Out of the blue, a black cat raced across the road. I slowed down to avoid hitting it. Normally I would turn my superstitious ass around to pick a different route, but I was focused on getting to this familiar pussy. I carried on convincing myself bad luck isn't real. I quickly got second thoughts as the police turned out behind me. Like the cat, they came out of nowhere. My nervous system broke down, I tried not to look suspicious but it's close to 1am, I was suspect by association of being black in Birmingham Michigan, I can tell they are running the license plate just by how they were following, keeping a short distance. Fortunately, it's Amber's car. After what seemed like forever at the stop light, they finally went around. I calmly maintained my position while glancing out my peripheral vision. The black cop looked at me as they drove past, a sense of relief came over me.

"Ol oreo ass nigga" I said to myself. I began singing the chorus to Kendrick Lamar's song "We gone be alright", before I realized, I was just lucky as hell. I cautiously made my way down the dark street where Kim lived. Once I arrived at her single-story ranch style house, her door was wide open and all I could see is a flashlight shining at me in circles as if someone was directing traffic.

I approached leisurely with my hand up blocking the light just to be sure it was her. The light pointed down once I got to the porch. She posed like an Instagram model in the doorway. She wore a silk black robe and red open toe heels that made her look both demanding and delectable. She opened the screen door and grabbed my shirt in the chest area with force pulling me closer to her. We tongue kissed delicately as she slid her way inside my jeans, grabbing my gentleman before walking backwards bringing me along with a serious look on her face. I had no doubts; I was confident the pleasure would be well worth the lie I told to get here. We made it to the kitchen, she pushed my back against the oven door.

I toyed with her a bit

"Damn baby you all feisty tonight what's up, I could use some sleep in that nice mattress firm bed y'all have."

"Whatever Derrick, now you know you're not getting any sleep tonight... plus I want to try something."

"Oh lord what is it?"

She laughed.

"Wouldn't you like to know, don't worry you're about to find out and maybe, just maybe I'll think about letting you share it with sister Amber, who's not really a sister, but I guess she can learn and do it for you at home."

"Aww, here you go throwing shade!"

"No, no babe, no shade, I just don't understand why they have to have our men too."

"Since when did it become white women verses black women or any woman, and why do you care?"

"Because it's a slap in the face to single good black women. I don't understand how our men can abandon us for the master's daughter, when we have the highest gift value, it's crazy that we depreciate so fast within the small pool of black men available in our own communities who aren't incarcerated. It's like we're good enough to lay with and impregnate, yet nothing more. But at the end of the day I just think she should take care of her man if she wants to keep him. You're a black king baby, but you can't be a king with a white chick -- sorry not sorry -- I'm just the messenger."

I shot her a crazy look.

"What do you mean by that and who's the sender Mrs. messenger?"

"Come on Derrick you know what I mean and if she's taking care of you fully why are you here twice a month? Obviously, something is lacking at home and we both know what it is. I know she don't get you right. I bet its always missionary style in the bedroom with the lights off or some shit."

"Okay so maybe your right but damn church lady why are you being so rude? Sounds like jealousy to me, I'm assuming the rules don't apply to you."

"I'm not married to a white man, am I? And I'm not at all jealous baby, when I want you, I have you..."

"Oh, you cocky huh?"

"Not at all, I just call it how I see it boo. Where do you tell her you're going this late anyway?"

"Shiiitt, sometimes I just leave or tell her I'm hanging

out with the fellas but if I think she is going to trip I just start an argument over something petty then leave. But she rarely asks, see that's one of the differences between black and white women, they don't harass a nigga, since we're getting all technical into race specifics. Little do you know Amber does have some black in her.

"Boy please that woman is white as snow."

"You know what I mean, like she has some good qualities that most black women have. "Okay name one?"

"Umm hold on let me think..."

"Naw, if she so black you shouldn't have to think about it, but I'll help you out. How does she cook chicken wings?"

"Huh… what does that have to do with anything?"

"Just tell me how she cooks them."

"She bakes them."

"No, I'm talking about her fried chicken wings."

"Um, just like anyone would, she pre-heats the air fryer, put this homemade parmesan seasoning on them, then put her flour in a pan…"

"Nope! AHHNTT wrong. All black people know you season the flour inside a plastic sack and shake it until the creases of the wings are covered. Welp, she's got your ass in the sunken place. The only black she's mixed with is you when you're in her, and like I said, I'm sure that's rare. But I will say, don't let her race fool you at the end of the day she's still a woman, trust me when I say she is no dummy, she knows what the hell you're out here doing. Just make sure she doesn't find out who you're doing it with! I have a reputation to uphold at church. I don't need no mess."

"Ayye I don't get caught!"

"That's what you speak now but remember Proverbs 6:31, "Yet if he is caught, he must pay seven-fold, tho it cost him all the wealth of his house." Derrick.... sometimes God spares no expense to lead you back to him and down the right path. So, if ever the shoe is on the other foot you can't complain."

"Okay, now I'm super confused. First you were dissing my wife now you're saying I shouldn't be cheating on her and you're the one who's sleeping with her husband."

She laughed aloud.

"True, true. Good point my bad I had a sista Kim holy moment for a minute, don't judge me."

"Okay, well can a sista suck a brutha's dick now?"

"Oh, hell nah. Sista Kim can't be doing all that. I just told you I had a reputation to protect, but nasty Kim can… hold on I got you boo."

"She pulled out hand cuffs from the kitchen drawer with a smile on her face.

"Come on now Kim I don't think that's a good idea this time."

"Oh, hush big baby it's all in fun, plus this will keep you from grabbing my bundles. You be tangling my shit up, trying to kill me with that big ass dick touching the back of my damn throat. I still have to breathe."

"Don't guilt me for being into it, you shouldn't do it so good."

I leaned back and went along with her little game, allowing her to cuff my wrist together behind my back.

"Ooo this is going to be interesting... now don't you go anywhere I'll be right back"

"Yeah very funny."

I knew she enjoyed roll play, but I was always iffy and on edge which sometimes made it hard to enjoy sex once we got around to it.

MOUTH HYPNOSIS

She came back into the kitchen like she never left.

She lifted my shirt to run her gel filled fingernails back and forth across my abs. She opened her robe exposing her fresh scented, raw model-like body, pulling me toward her by the buckle of my belt. She hopped on me locking her arms around my neck, and her legs around my waistline. We continued the kissing session that we paused earlier at the door. I wanted so bad to palm her small ass cheeks but settled for watching them rest on the granite island where I leaned in to place her. I shifted to her neck, rushing to reach her thick maple brown nipples that seemed to call me by my first name. Eventually, I connected with her shea buttered breasts, devouring them slow with detail, they were perfect and always better than advertised, soft and fulfilling. I gave each titty a fair share of my mouth's lubricant, she put her arm around the back of my head applying presser, I knew she was ready to receive me, and I had a gift for her. She laid back on the counter with her legs spread watching my head descend, the tip of my tongue lingered at the lower end of her pussy. I ran it inside her gap, separating her walls with my no hand technique. I fell into a pussy eating coma with rhythm, pacing my flow to be consistent with her moans.

"Oh my god, just like that Derrick!"

She put her hands on each side of my face pulling my ears then disconnecting me from her wet faucet to meet her eye level, kissing the moisture from her pink source off my lips.

"Whew shoot. Damn, I forgot how talented you are with that mouth, Jesus!"

She hoped down and went to pull out a brown paper sack from the cabinet.

"Here, I stopped by the store and got you something."

She reached inside the bag and took out some airheads.

"Girl you didn't stop and get nothing you been had

these, probably bought them for your Sunday school kids, but I'll take them, thank you."

"You're a brat, so ungrateful yet you have no clue."

"Clue, girl whatever."

I grabbed one with my teeth attempting to remove the wrapper, she snatched it.

"Whoa what are you doing sir?"

"About to eat it, what you mean, you said they were for me."

"Yeah they are for you, but they're not for you, for you, they're for you to use with me."

"Huh? You are confusing the hell out of me... How many glasses of wine did you have? Because you're making no sense at all..."

"Watch."

She took her heels off and bent to her knees unfastening my belt. She unzipped my jeans with her lips.

"Hey big boy there you are."

She said, talking to my best friend like I wasn't standing there. It turned me on to watch her hold it like a microphone, raising it up to suck on my freshly shaved balls. She toyed with it before attaching the expandable cherry flavor candy like a splint to my main vain.

"Am I making more sense now?"

"Much more…. auu shuuu –"

I couldn't respond fast enough; she abandoned the small talk to fill her mouth. Her saliva and the candy together created a red stream on the way to the floor. With every reckless slurp she took, she made a large portion of the airhead disappear. We were both anxious to fuck. She climbed back on me like I was a tree. Her warm, wet pussy pressed against my lower abdomen. She clenched her teeth on my collarbone and traced my ear with her tongue. She began guiding me to the bedroom. My pants fell around my ankles with her clinging to my body as if I was about to pull her to safety, I bumped into several things including her foyer table knocking something over.

"Go, keep going I'll get it later."

We got to her room and didn't bother shutting the door.

"Right here"

"Where?"

"Right here on the dresser"

She bit my lip than kissed my chest area reaching her hands around to remove the cuffs. I propped my dick up and slid the beast inside, gripping her little booty like it mattered, pulling her closer to stuff more in. I almost wanted to say I love you; her pussy was so good.

"Fuck, you got some good pussy, shit."

I choked her neck pinning her face against the mirror as I drifted this pipe in and out of her core.

"Oouu, God I like yo dick in me! Mhmm biiig, deeeep dick, yes -- don't stop baby" she moaned. I went faster letting air in, her pussy farted as I pounded it out.

"Damn Kim, ouu I'm about to cum, shit yo pussy too good!"

"Mmm no wait please not yet baby!"

It was too late her sexy ass moan caused a roar of nut to erupt from me. I barely pulled out and I had more than plenty to offer. I squeezed the rest out of the tip of my dick with my thumb, releasing it on the outskirts of her clit.

"Damn girl whew.

The protein cream rolled down in between her legs on to the dresser.

"So, you couldn't hold it five more minutes?"

"You were taking too long girl, it's not my fault you got some lava in there." She pushed me back on to the bed.

"Whatever you owe me, and I want it tonight."

"Damn you so bossy, I like it though, what if I can't get it back up?"

"Don't worry, that's my job. I'll get him back up, trust me…"

ROUND TWO

We laid up for about half an hour, watching animal planet as she crunched on ice. It wasn't too long before her nymphomania disorder kicked in without warning. I assumed the lions getting it in set her off. She grabbed a mouth restraint.

"You ready?"

"Whoa hol --" is all I could say before she sealed my lips shut with a devilish laugh. "Huh? What's was that?... I can't understand you."

She reached for the feather handcuffs on the dresser and re-cuffed my wrists. It was something about being in control that stimulated her. She spit on my dick and starts sucking me up aggressively, adding ice to the action. Kim moaned as if it brought more pleasure to her and looked at me each time she came up for air.

"Are you enjoying this?"

"um mm hmm.." I mumbled barely able to respond.

Her phone lit up before vibrating its way off the nightstand and onto the floor. She climbed over me in a hurry reaching down off the side of the bed.

"Hello" she answered, out of breath.

"Oh, hey babe..." she trailed. She reversed her way over me back into position putting him on speaker sitting the phone on top of me right above my dick area returning to assignment. She was sucking the strength out of me. Marcel started talking about how their short staff again, with it still in her mouth she said "Awwe I'm sorry honey that sucks."

Baby are you eating something... He asked. "Yea boo, just some ice."

"Oh, you love that ice, don't you?" She raised up to get something as they held a conversation.

"Yeah, I can't help it honey that's one habit I will have to pray about, because this addiction here, let me tell you...Are you doing alright? Is your back feeling okay?"

Knowing her husband well enough to know that questions would just trigger him to ramble on about pure nothing, which is just what she wanted giving her time to multitask between listening and bobbing her head up and down on my stiff dick. She tried her best not to slurp too hard, giving long smooth strokes shaking it inside her mouth against her tongue ring. At times she just sucked on my balls and rubbed the chocolate stick down with her saliva while responding to Marcel. After a while boredom set in, overshadowing her ability to listen effectively, she started to cross the line testing my manhood by sliding her fingers close to my ass hole. I wiggled around with wide eyes looking down at her with a "stop fucking playing" look on my face. She covered her mouth to keep her loud ass laugh from spilling over.

"Well honey bun, I was just calling to check on you because I knew you were up. You know your school classes will be starting up here soon, you may want to start forcing yourself to sleep so you can be in the routine when it's time to go back."

"Yeah I know I will definitely make this my last week of late nights and early mornings because I do be tired."

"Well I have about five minutes left before the assembly belt starts back up, I'm going to try and down this chicken and rice that you packed for me."

"Aw, ok baby." she said in a long mournful voice as if

she wished he had more time. "Oh hey, Mookie, have you seen that black box I had sitting on top of the table?"

"That meter device looking thingy? Last I remember, you took it to your truck that day you said you were helping Carl."

"Dang I could have sworn...."

"Marcell! Don't swear honey!"

"I'm sorry sweetie, I mean, I thought I seen it there last. I guess I'll have to look for it some more when I get off."

"Yeah probably so babe."

"Okay then."

I shook my head at her impatiently. He was fucking up my concentration. Once they disconnected, I muttered, "*finally*" loud enough for her to hear...

"What was that ... you want to be sexually assaulted? Oou I almost forgot; I owe you a birthday gift. ...and I just happen to have one grapefruit left, you are so lucky Mr." She was talking to me as if I could speak back. Leaving me in the room looking like I had been abducted.

KIM

I went to the kitchen to prepare what I like to call a pleasure platter. Good is deep in me, as is the Lord. I know my husband didn't deserve to have another man in his playpen, time and time again. He is beyond good and wonderful to me. He works hard and very supportive of my goals. He doesn't cheat and he rubs my feet. There wasn't much more that I could ask for in a man, but I liked what I like. The best thing I could do was conceal my imperfections.

Derrick is the center of my sin. I love fucking the sperm out of this man and did so like he belonged to me. As I alter this fruit, I thought about how wet my pink purse gets at church whenever I see that white woman standing next to his fine ass. Not knowing that I carry a mental map of his third curved leg it's like I can feel him inside me during service. I ventured so deep in thought, it almost slipped my mind that he was in my bed waiting for me. I hurried back to him.

"Well, well… I didn't keep you to long did I?"

I watched him watching me looking helpless, he knew I was in control.

"Aww, you went back down on me, I'm sad now." I

said revealing the grapefruit. I talked to him softly.

"Don't worry we can fix this. Although, I must admit I'm not crazy about grapefruit, I brought some caramel too, I hope you don't mind."

I played with his limp piece of artwork until it woke back up. "You know they say grapefruits are somewhat like a vagina...how the muscles are tight in the beginning, then loosens up from the moisture when a woman is turned on."

"If I slide my tongue in and out of this grapefruit the juice pockets will bust giving off moisture allowing it to open vastly, pretty unique I know."

He gave me a look as if I were crazy, that's when I put my mouth on it and gave him a few long strokes of head before sliding his brown mamba through the make-shift hole of the fruit. He sighed and twisted a bit from the shock of chill it held, I giggled.

"oh, I'm sorry that's another difference I failed to mention, it starts out a little cold before it gets warm... you'll be alright big baby." I squeezed the caramel inside the hole then sucked the head of what remained sticking out. The sopping juices from me squeezing the fruit flowed down to his balls, it didn't take long for me to chase, siphoning it up as fast as it came down. The stokes

47

got intense, his legs kicked wildly showing the level of intensity as he shot nut in the air. His squirming body was close to being free, I reclaimed it by placing my mouth back on the tip. His eyes began to water from me sucking what was left out of his sensitive penis, his fist and toes were curled by the time I got done. I uncuffed his hands and removed the gag ball from his mouth.

"Damn you trying to kill a nigga tonight huh. Whew shit, got damn"

"Never! I just wanted to be sure I got it all."

I threw him a soapy towel.

"Oh, and just like sex you must be sure to wash up good because you could get a serious infection."

He washed up then wiped his ass free of the uncomfortable moisture that lingered. I was ready to park my wet pussy on his big juicy lips again. I went all in, reversing my cat woman on his face. He knew just what I wanted. Receiving her with his mouth wide open, he spread my ass cheeks apart to dig as deep as he could go. His cheek bones met my thick round ass, I gripped the bed twerking my second set of lips back and forth on his bearded face. He rubbed his thumb on my wrinkled clit for several minutes.

I yanked forward and squirted all over him, clinching his ankles, I sucked on his big toe until I came to a drip. I was at ease placing my head down on the bed between his legs.

PILLOW TALK

We were motionless for minutes just embracing the glory of alleviating ourselves.

"Well that was fun how often do you release like that, my goodness."

I laughed.

"Oh hush, don't judge me... just know you never dissatisfy."

"I'm just saying, that was some intense stuff. That's the first time I've actually seen you bust like that. You almost shot my eye out!"

"That's because you never eat my cat. It's always us fucking or me sucking... Hell, my own husband doesn't get the attention I give you. So yes, I made it a priority to put it all in your face tonight, my lady likes attention too."

"Well hey you never ask, so I figured you just like giving head"

"Oh, trust me I do enjoy comforting an energized penis, but I love -- no, I take that back I love God, but I really enjoy head."

"Well you have to speak up."

"Come on Derrick that's like a mutual thing, if I do you, then you should be kind enough to return the favor, it's selfish for you not to."

"Maybe so, I was just always taught that a closed mouth doesn't get fed."

"Well that mouth was plenty open tonight and got fed really good, guess I'll be washing tonight. If Marcel see's this mess it will be world war three."

"Hey, it's ok if you get caught but for God's sake, just don't let him catch who you're doing it with, remember!"

"I thought we were in this together!?"

"We weren't in it together when you told me not to get caught..."

"Child hush nobody's getting caught."

"Well just to be sure, what time did you say he gets here?"

"Maybe about five, five-thirtyish."

"You do know it's four forty-seven

"I know I got this. Why are you in a rush to leave me?"

"What do you mean Kim, do you see what time it is? Marcel probably leaving work now if he hasn't left already!"

"No, he hasn't. I know my husband and he loves to talk. If anything, he is running his mouth with coworkers, trust me. You can lay with me for a little while before you go."

"Alright but only ten minutes."

"Fifteen?" she begged.

"Okay, fifteen minutes that's it. You forget I have a wife to answer too also."

"I know but she will be alright. I only get to have you a few times a month, if that."

I laid my head on his chest, crossing my leg over his, sweeping them up and down.

"What's on your mind?"

"Nothing just tired. What's on yours?"

"Oh, something but nothing."

"Huh what does that mean?"

"It means I have something on my mind, but don't know if I should say…" she trailed.

"Oookay then, next subject shall we."

"No, Derrick. Stop it! You're supposed to either assume or ask me what it is that I'm

thinking not just disregard it silly."

"Okay so, I'm on a game show? Yeah see if nothing else all women have this in common y'all expect us to know what you're thinking, when you're thinking it, and it's strange that y'all don't ever know what the hell y'all want. Not to eat, or anything. Then? -- it's always nothing when it's really something. I promise y'all are like cellphones without signal, just lost, now if you don't just say what's on your mind..."

"I was just thinking about that thing we did..."

"We've done a lot of things you have to be more specific."

"Okay, to be more specific that very nasty thing we did with your friend when we first started messing around."

"Who Jazz? What my dick not good enough by itself?"

"It's nothing like that Derrick. It just felt so good pleasing two men at the same time knowing one is slamming his hard dick in my mouth and the other is beating my spine. I like the nonstop action; do you know how hard I cum having a dick in my ass and another one in my pussy at the same time? That feeling is everything.

"That sounds about right." he joked.

"Oh hush!" I said, hoping he understood.

"But for real, you know I told you Jazz be busy working that night shift, he sleeps all day and barely has time to hang out with me."

"Well what about that white guy that you and Amber use to come to church with? He was kind of cute."

"Who, Seth? I'm not getting down with her brother like that! Hell naw!"

"Well my bad dang. I didn't know that was her brother. Why did he stop coming?"

"Oh, so now you want some rare meat after clowning me... Now look at you. If you must know, his kind of cute ass has an alcohol addiction. Amber thought that church and counseling would help him, but it didn't he was doing good for a while though. I don't know why people think God is always the answer to all their problems."

"Because he is Derrick! What, do you not believe that?"

"To be honest sometimes I don't know what to believe I personally have never seen God, or the holy spirit, have you?"

"Everyone knows that you walk by faith and not by sight, God is in you, so you have the power to create the best outcome for your life through the choices you make. But right now, let us not talk about the life choices while we're committing adultery... it's not fair to the God in me, I'm just saying. "

"Hey fine by me I don't even remember how we got on the topic, but I do know that I'm getting sleepy."

"Well, let's return to the original conversation... we were trying to find someone to have a threesome with remember?"

"No. You were trying to find someone. I was listening and that's not a threesome that's a train."

"It's the same difference!... it's three people either way."

"Oh, it makes a difference. When two hammers are involved it's always a train... it's only a threesome when its two women and one man"

"How the hell did you come up with that?"

"Because for it to be a threesome, all parties must interact which means I'm fucking you; she's kissing me while you are eating her, that's a threesome. Trust me, I'm not sucking no dick, no ma'am, no ham, no turkey."

"So, you're not going to help me daddy?"

"I don't know anyone, especially someone close enough for me to feel comfortable bumping dicks with.

Even if I needed help, which I don't, but hypothetically speaking if I did, Jazz is probably the only person I would consider doing that with. But hey since we're being so open, I have a random question."

"What?"

"Have you ever engaged with pastor?"

"What? Oh God no!"

"Would you ever?"

"Heck no, why would you ask that? Have you lost your mind? That's like the closest you get to God. An ordained minister? Oh no baby, that's a sure ticket purchased to hell in advance, one way with no lights. No sir, I will not be Eve. What did Corinthians 10:21 say? I believe it was, "He cannot drink the cup of the Lord, and the cup of Devil". don't quote me but it's something like that. Either way I'm drinking from one cup; I don't do germs boo."

"Okay sister Mary dang!"

"You do know that Mary was Jesus' mother?"

"I know she wasn't no virgin. Mary was probably out there being ratchet, getting it in, got pregnant and didn't know who her baby daddy was."

"Boy shut yo crazy self up!"

"No for real if God made all things, there is nothing wrong with getting the pastors rocks off, he's just a man like me."

THE CLOSE CALL

I tapped him in the chest then raised up knowing our time was sure to expire, I saw the sun peeking through the blinds. I grabbed his hand pulling him toward me, he stood up with open arms wrapping them around me kissing on my neck.

"Too bad we're out of time huh?"

"Well there's always another night but come on you have to go; Marcell will be here any minute."

We made way out the bedroom to the entryway. I looked out the peep hole then cracked the door open wide enough to stick my head out looking both ways. Just as I was about to push him out, I saw car lights approaching and knew they were Marcell's aftermarket Chevy truck lights.

"Hold up this might be him!"

"Yep it is! Oh my goodness!"

"No, Kim don't do that...stop playing! Are you serious!?"

I didn't respond. It didn't take long for him to comprehend that I wasn't playing.

"What happened to, *"he likes to talk"* ... I guess not today huh?! You know I can't get caught in here right... looks like we gotta kill him! Do u have a knife, a gun, or something?! I know you got something around here for his big ass just in case he ever tried to put his gorilla hands on you. We need that shit right now!"

"Huh... What, calm yo ass down. Nobody is killing nobody -- just let me think!"

"Well good cause it's happy hour at Pure Lounge tonight with half price wings and nachos. So, what's the plan?"

"I'm not about to play with you right now."

I shut the door and turned on the alarm. With an unsettled look on his face he asked. "Why you do that?"

"Because if the alarm isn't on, then he's going to know something isn't right, he's big, not dumb.

"Well at least he's Christian."

"When it comes to me, he's crazy..."

"I'm just gone act gay then, tell him we were sipping wine, or some shit cause a bitch like me need my life."

"Would you stop and be serious, this is what's going to happen: he's going to pull in the garage, when he turns off the alarm to come in, I will open the door and you get the hell out."

"Don't say *get the hell out* like you didn't invite me over here, what about --"

"The alarm is disabled! Go, go!" I shoved him out the screen door, catching it not to slam, he ran to the car, looking guilty as hell.

DERRICK

My heart was racing about the same speed I was driving to beat the sun home. It clearly had a head start on me. I made myself aware of the speed limit, slowing down some. I let off the accelerator a little more before getting to the nearest gas station. I got stuck using this irritating gas pump that repeatedly stopped after dispersing small amounts of fuel. It seemed like it took forever just to pump twelve dollars' worth, but I struggled through it just to avoid hearing Ambers mouth. I pulled out joining early morning traffic, jamming to a pop station. I felt great about the day until I made it just a few blocks away from home and spotted a state sheriff sitting off to the side near an abandoned retail store, lurking. It was like he was waiting on my ass.

I drove past flawlessly, I thought. A delay of his American lights struck me from behind, my stomach fell into a knot once he pointed that super bright light in the car. I pondered during our unreasonable standstill thinking about what excuse I could use for driving while suspended. After moments of sitting, his door finally opened, he examined the vehicle carefully, while approaching with his hand on his gun, I kept my hands visible so there was no misunderstanding.

"Good morning Sir, coming from work or heading to work?"

"I'm getting off my second job, headed home to get ready for the first one."

"Well the reason why I stopped you is because your lights weren't on. Can you tell me why that is?"

I know he was just being an ass hole with intentions to fuck with me.

"Sir it's not dark out, the sun is up and normally this car has auto-light. I guess my wife must have had the auto function turned off." I said calmly.

"I understand, so this is your wife's car?"

"Yes sir."

"Do you have identification and insurance?"

"Yes sir, it's probably in the glove box or under in this arm rest."

"Okay well go ahead and hand me your license and see if you can find that insurance card. When you find it, hold it out the window and I'll come grab it from you," he assured.

"Yes sir."

I took the risk of giving him my license knowing the situation wasn't going to end well. I prepared myself for his findings. He sat in the car with his door wide open, in the course of searching for Amber's insurance, I came across a bullet vibrator in the shape of lipstick hiding underneath papers in the armrest.

What the fuck, I said to myself, *oh we're addressing this*. Once I found the insurance papers, I stuck it out the window thinking more about the mini toy than the fate of my freedom. The sheriff gradually walked back over, inspecting the insurance card, verifying that it matched the VIN.

"And you're Derrick Ross correct?"

"Yes sir."

"Okay well here's the deal Derrick -- your license is suspended and has been for some time now. You also have a couple of warrants coming back out of Southfield."

I hurried to plead my case, but the sheriff stopped me before I could begin.

"Hold on now, let me finish before you jump off the deep end. I'm going to give you a warning, but you do need to get both of those taken care of. I technically should be towing this car and taking you to jail."

I quickly replied, "yes sir" and shared how appreciative I was.

"Alright here you go" he said, handing back my belongings, making me feel like a child with his last remark.

"I hope this is a good start to your day, be sure to buckle up."

"Thank you officer and will do. I appreciate the warning."

I did just what he said and buckled my black ass up before we parted ways. I drove off with his lights glaring in my rearview mirror. I made it home right before any of my realistic excuses could seem like an expired lie. Smothering myself in deep breaths of relief, I sat there until the dings from the car's door sensor got the best of my patients.

No Security in Insecurity

Quiet as can be I tip-toed my way up our loud, squeaky-only-at-night stairs. I was surprised to see that Amber was still out. I crawled across our room floor to her side of the bed. I quietly patted the beds surface until I felt her charger cable that lead to her phone, wedge underneath her elbow. I worked carefully to free it without disturbing her, I snuck out the room using a dirty shirt from our hamper to smother the phones volume while turning it to vibrate. I sat on the toilet combing through it thoroughly, finding nothing to offset my minor guilt. After running into a dead end on her social media, I washed my dick off then went to kiss her face and neck creating a mild distraction to replace it...

"Derrick... stop. What are you doing? What time is it?" she managed sleepily.

She looked at her phone.

"Oh no, I'm going to be late!" She hurried up to get herself together I laid in the spot she got up from.

"Oh no you don't! Get up! I need you to take Ashley to daycare, I'll pack her bag and while you're at it, go ahead and pay the dues for next month so we don't get behind again."

A few hours later not realizing that I fell asleep, I woke in a cold sweat frantically searching for my phone, knowing I got shit in there that will instantly turn a logical thinking spouse to lose their fucking mind. I found it face down under the cover and searched all my apps to see if anything was out of place. Nothing stood out that would indicate it was tampered with, yet I knew my wife was no fool. I knew she could be slicker than ice, any woman who takes pictures of the dirt in your phone from her phone, then send that shit to you after a series of questions that you already lied about, is dangerous. It's almost scary to think about, fortunately I was running behind and had no time to think.

A Father's Heart

Ashley was watching tv in her room without a worry in the world. I sometimes wished I could shield her from the harsh troubles of life that I knew she would one day discover.

"Come on babe, we have to go and why are you so close to the tv?" I asked her lovingly.

"Go where daddy?"

"You know you have daycare and I have work boo."

"Aw I don't wanna go daddy!"

"Me either pumpkin face, but it's the only way mommy and I can buy that kitty stuff and all those shammy dolls you like."

"Aww my head hurts daddy"

"I know what will fix that how about some cookies, cookies fix everything right?"

"But mommy say's no snacks before real food."

"Well guess what? Mommy isn't here, so it can be our secret unless you tell on me, are you going to tell on your daddy?"

She shook her head no.

"Good you better not, or else..." I said jokingly in a kid manner.

"Or else what daddy?"

"Youuu get the claw!"

"No!"

I grabbed her little belly tickling her until she curled up in a ball.

"Okay, okay babe we really need to go... here put these black shoes on."

"But I wanna wear these..." She pointed to some shoes I knew damn well her mother would harass me about later, but I approved anyway... We got situated in the car. It wasn't until I was halfway to Ashley's day care center before I realized I didn't grab my lunch.

"Damn!"

"Awww that's a bad word daddy"

"Sorry baby, you're right don't you say it."

"Okay"

"You remember the big three?"

"Yes"

"Okay let's hear it always be..."

"Kind."

"Never let them see you..."

"Cry."

"If anyone mess with you…"

"Tell Daddy."

"That's my girl. Okay now let's get you in here."

At that moment she got uncomfortably sad. Once I parked the car, she spoke.

"Well Mr. Sneed, sometimes…" she lingered.

"Huh? Mr. Sneed what...Ashley I'm talking to you! What did he do? He touches you, hits you, what is it?"

She remained quiet. I called Amber, she sent me straight to voicemail followed by an **"I'm busy"** text. We went inside, and I stood at the sign-in desk waiting to speak to someone. then his fruity ass come around the corner all cheerful

"Hey Mr. Ross!"

I ran over and snatched his pussy ass up with belligerence.

"Fuck nigga you been touching my daughter?!"

He looked rightfully startled.

"What are you talking about?"

"Don't act dumb now!"

Security saved his ass before I could stomp a hole in his face. Using force to separate me from him, I heard an officer say, "Sir calm down."

They pulled me in an office room.

"What's going on sir?"

"Y'all got some motherfucking pedophiles working here that's what's going on, my daughter told me. He's doing shit he shouldn't be when it comes to a child!"

"Could you be more specific?"

"Nigga how much more........."

In the middle of my rage walked in the daycare director.

"Good morning Mr. Ross, what's the problem?"

"The problem is somebody is not doing their damn job when it comes to my child's safety!" I said looking at the security guards while I spoke. The director looked dumbfounded.

"Mr. Ross what are you implying?"

"What I'm saying is something isn't right. My baby girl is not going to say that someone is messing with her inappropriately for no reason."

"How old is Ashley sir?"

"What the hell does that matter? Are you implying that I'm lying? I will have the state in here shutting your ass down!"

"No, Mr. Ross. I'm not saying that you are, however, sometimes kids say things out of context or in a manner which most adults would interpret differently from what is intended."

"Ashley has been acting a lot strange here lately. She doesn't focus and her behavior has been off as well. Now I have spoken with Mr. Sneed and he has agreed not to press charges."

"Press charges?! Oh, y'all really doing the foo, call the punk ass police and let's see how they feel about this. If my baby has been acting different from what you're use to maybe that should be considered a sign that something is wrong wouldn't you agree?"

"I assure you that we will be doing a full investigation because those are serious accusations. Our top priority is the safety and the wellbeing of every kid here, but due to this incident today we can't accept Ashley here anymore."

"Well good because she wasn't staying anyway!"

I walked out holding Ashley close. Moments later Amber called.

72

"What the hell Derrick!? What is your problem?"

"What do you mean, *my* problem?"

"The daycare called telling me how you went in there acting a plum foo, you know they can kick us out permanently for that right? What the fuck babe? What are you thinking?"

"If my baby girl tells me that someone has been touching her inappropriately, you think I'm not going to say anything?"

"Have you lost the good part of your damn mind Derrick?!"

"Did she tell you that in those exact words Derrick?"

"No, -- but"

"—Exactly! That girl just says stuff that's what kids do. You can't go in there putting your hands on people without exploring to see if there's any truth behind what's been shared. You have to do your due diligence, then act accordingly, like a fucking adult! Got me all out of character at work because you wanna act senseless."

"You done? Hello? Hello!?"

She hung up before I could return fire. I called back three times before she finally answered.

"Yes Derrick!"

"You weren't going to let me defend myself, just hang

up huh."

"I am at work. This is not the time or place we will definitely have this discussion at home."

"Well can you call your mom and see if she can watch Ashley until you get off?"

"No, I will not because you don't think about things before you act on them. You just make decisions in that peanut ass head of yours and go with it. So you figure it out goodbye!"

Knowing I couldn't afford to miss any more days of work, I got desperate and texted Kim.

Hey, Kim, what are you up to I need a big favor.

I quickly retracted...

Never mind it's okay.

Knowing I can't take my child to a chick I'm fucking. I texted Jazz.

Aye I need a favor like asap.

He replied instantly.

What's good?

Bro I need you to watch Ash until I get off.

You already know...

"*You already know*" was code for "anything for my nigga, **okay bet.**"

Slide thru. Nia and Jayla can watch her they didn't

**have school today you know I'm going to be sleep until
it's time for us to link up, but we here.**

Cool I'll be there in 10 minutes.

Okay.

I pulled up rushing to get her inside.

"Hey Nia!"

"Were at uncle Jazz daddy?!"

"Yeah I know boo"

Jazz was sitting on the porch with his girls. Ashley
climbed the stairs meeting Jayla halfway.

"Aye bro good looking! I know that night shift kicking
yo ass huh?"

"Man... Hell yeah! Easy money tho." he laughed.

"I bet, put me on?"

"You be on that bull; you know I will in a heartbeat.
Ya boy could use that referral money."

"All day though, I gotta get out of here. I'll have
Amber pick her up when she gets off."

"Aye I got them thangs for y'all too. I'll give the card
to Amber."

"Bet! You know we need them. Our refrigerator looks like it had bypass surgery. The other day I opened it and it said *what are you here for*!"

"You a nut, get to work dawg!"

"I'll catch you tonight bro."

SAME SHIT, DIFFERENT DAY

I finally made it to work, arriving way past my scheduled start time. I gathered my thoughts so that the lie I told for being late would be consistent. I took it a step further and rubbed both of my hands on the back of my inner tire, wiping the black debris on my pants giving myself that authentic, I-really-changed-out-a-tire look. Only because I know how Ms. Lori likes to play a detective and shit.

When I walked in, it felt like a free day. The office staff was chilling along with Issac and Jeremy, the groundskeeper.

"Damn! Y'all way too comfortable aren't y'all? What are you smiling for Issac?"

"Because your boss-man-lady isn't here yet... that's why we're all chilling my brotha."

"So, you mean to tell me I came up with this good ass lie for nothing?"

"Apparently, hey save whatever excuse it was for next time."

"Well I'm out before she does get here. I have work to do."

"Man, you don't have shit to do! I know because I don't have shit to do."

"Issac shut yo bean head ass up, see that's your problem. You too damn friendly with these office hoes. One week they jeffing with you, the next week you're getting written up. Who you think snitching?! Be smart and hide out like I'm about to do big dog."

"Chill they coo bro, hell I could tell on them too!"

"Yeah okay do you."

I hid out in a vacant apartment unit for most of the day. Amber texted me that afternoon.

"So where did you take our daughter this morning?"

I decided to pull her leg for leaving me in a tough

position.

"I took her to your sister's."

"You did what?! Don't play with me!"

"What was I supposed to do? You left me hanging, I had no choice."

"So, you left my child with that basic hoe?"

I couldn't respond quick enough, she called in the middle of my text.

"I know you're playing with me, right? You must be playing!"

"Why are you tripping? That basic hoe is still your sister."

"She stopped being my sister when her and my biological father started messing around. Now stop playing with me Derrick!"

"Okay, chill out. She's good, I took her over to Jazz house. You can pick her up over there when you wrap up. And get that food card from him so we can go shopping after work."

"You almost got jacked up."

I let her ramble on, then I asked a question that would confirm if she looked through my phone or not.

"Hey where did you put my earpiece? It was sitting on top of my phone."

"I don't know, I didn't touch it. But I have to go, you know some people actually work." she joked.

"How do you know I'm not working?"

"What are you doing Derrick?"

"Chilling."

"My point. Bye! I gotta go. I will pick her up after I leave the daycare from fixing your fuck up."

I was about to take a nap to kill the last couple hours of the day when Ms. Lori caught my attention over the walkie-talkie radio.

"Hey, Derrick, can you come to the office?"

I managed to avoid her ass all day now she wanted to talk. I made my way to her office.

"Hey, what's going on boss lady?"

"Ooh nothing but something."

"It's always that something huh?"

"You betcha and that something just happens to be the air not working in apartment 109. I know it's close to quitting time and I'm sure you guys are itching to get out of here, but we can't leave a resident without air. It's really warm out. Perhaps you and Issac can team up to get it fixed and still be out by five thirty or so. That ok?"

"No problem Ms. Lori."

"Perfect! Also, if you need anything have Megan call

me. I'll be heading out early, my significant other and I have dinner arrangements. See you guys tomorrow!"

"You enjoy that, but you definitely won't see me tomorrow."

"Huh, what do you mean?" she said with a confused look on her face, playing stupid like she didn't know my off days.

I played along stroking her ego, highlighting her authority. Like I was her slave.

"I'm off on Tuesday's Ms. Lori, remember?"

"Ohh that's right! Well enjoy your day off. I'll see you Wednesday."

Issac and I met up about fifteen minutes later.

ISSAC

I was about to clock out when Derrick yelled my name.

"Aye, Issac! Hold up bro. We still have some work to do."

"What you mean? It's about that time bruh..."

"Yo boss wants us to check out this ac unit before we clock out."

"Aw here y'all go with that end of the day shit and I was here on time!..."

"Hey, I'm just the messenger my friend."

"Well hurry yo ass up, I'm ready to get out of here."

"You just lazy, but I'm with it, because ya boy off tomorrow."

"You always off, I know you been hiding out the hole day looking at meme's and shit while I been out here busting my ass. Every five minutes her manly ass is calling my damn name on the radio."

Derrick instantly bust out laughing like I was playing.

"Aye I been busting my ass too." he said panting.

I gave him the side eye, with my lips stretched out to the same side.

"Yeah okay nigga, you don't have to front. I'm not Ms. Lori... I know you. What's up with her anyway? I saw her car pulling out, must be nice to came in late and leave early."

"Not sure. She told me she had plans with her significant other."

"Oh shit, you know her ass fruitier than starbursts."

"Man shut up! You don't know that woman's life."

"Dude I'm telling you she's not a dick taker, she's a strap on type of gal. Look at how she dresses... Now what woman do you know wear boots with Levi jeans in a business setting? Don't worry I'll wait... Plus she's using gay people choice of words, most people be like my husband or my girlfriend. Only people who's not comfortable with sharing their sexuality say shit like significant other. That means one thing, they don't want you to know they butt fucking or coochie bumping. And quite frankly, I don't give a damn if she's licking racoon ass."

"Issac you a foo bro!"

"It is what it is..."

The Plan

"For real I'm about ready to quit. Yesterday these muthafuckas were shooting broad daylight, scaring the damn cats!"

"Man fuck them damn cats! I thought you was about to say the kids!"

"Yeah them too...... I'm just tired bro. I'm tired of this job and her incompetent ass. I been with this company for three years and haven't seen a nickel extra."

"Well if you stop using these residents' bathrooms maybe they'll give you a little extra."

"Man, that was a one-time thing. What was I supposed to do, shit on myself?"

"Um let me see... Try making it to the office would

85

have been a more appropriate move player."

"Hey, this is chess, I was moving wisely. That Mexican spot tore my stomach up. Trust me, it wasn't my intentions for her to come home and see my big ass sitting on her toilet. I'll never forget that day, I had to use my shirt to wipe."

"I know you didn't think she was going to let you use her toilet paper too."

"We should have our own restroom anyway! I mean, why are we the only ones around here who have to arrange a time to release our bowels? Real talk, this work shit is becoming a lot like prison. They give us an identification number and a uniform to let everyone know we're their property for eight hours."

Derrick laughed.

"See you laughing but I'm telling you D, we need to come up with a strategic plan, a plan that's going to make us some real money man."

"You're a plain nut! What type plan you have in mind?"

"Hell, I don't know exactly, but it has to be a necessity, something people can't live without. Like a resource...... Like housing! Everyone needs somewhere to live. Or hey -- we could open a phone company. Phones are becoming a need nowadays bruh."

"Issac, you got a million dollars to start a phone company? I don't need to check my bank account to tell you that I don't."

"That's why we need a business loan."

"Oh, so you have good credit? Because again, I sure as hell don't."

"But your wife probably does."

"How you figure? Because she's white? All white people don't have good credit bruh, matter of fact my wife has black credit."

"I'm just saying. Oooohh I got it! Nigga I got it! We can open a hair cutting service."

"What... a barber shop? See now you just sound desperate. Everybody is cutting hair, braiding hair, gluing hair, sewing hair, making hair... They're even putting mustaches on eyelids now. I'm sure it's safe to say that lane is sewed up already."

"Nah, not like us. See nigga this would be a hair cutting service called "The Final Cut" for the deceased."

Derrick busted out laughing so hard, tears started to form in the creases of his eyes.

"What's funny? I'm not joking."

"I'm sorry, you're an idiot dog. I'm not cutting no dead

people's hair. I can't wait to tell Jazz this one. Aw man, I can't lie... yo ass is the main reason I keep coming to this damn place. You can't quit on me. I don't know how yo girl deal with you every day." He said laughing.

"Think about it. There are only two things guaranteed in life -- that's change and death. Everyone eventually dies, right? We might as well benefit from it. And correction.... it's all about how I deal with her bi-polar ass. I be ready to chop her in the throat but that wouldn't work. You know women who wear wigs got some strong necks carrying around extra weight."

"Man, y'all toxic! All y'all do is argue dog."

"She pisses me off sometimes. To the point I'm starting to become a petty nigga. The other day I took all her earring backs and put them in her favorite cereal."

"Man, if yo ass don't shut up and knock on this door."

"I'm not playing, and why the hell do I always have to knock?"

"Just in case they got dogs."

"Oh, you want me to get bit?"

"No. You're the dog lover! I see the way you be petting these resident's flea infested pets. Plus, you know damn well I don't do nobody's dog bruh. They unpredictable."

I knocked, "Maintenance!"

"-- Okay welp, they not here, let's go!"

Derrick laughed as I headed for the stairs then the door opened. He tried to recover back to a professional manner.

"I'm sorry is your mom home or someone who's over the age of eighteen?"

"I'm twenty." The young lady said.

"Oh, I'm sorry you look much younger, can I see your ID?"

"Sure"

She was halfway into her purse before Derrick's flirting started.

"I'm kidding you're cute enough, I believe you. Although you do look young, just how I like them."

"Oh, well thank you that's a good thing, I hope. My cousin has been expecting you guys. What took so long? Y'all got us all hot in here. That means she get half off her rent next month, right?"

"We're just the reefs in the ocean, you have to take that up with the sharks, but we will fix your air for free.", I said.

"Oh, the big one got jokes. I was just playing anyway. We know they cheap asses not giving anything out for free, but them stale ass peppermints in that candy bowl."

"Whoaa, what you mean the big one? And not too much on our peppermints.", I said.

"Well dang here's one reason you guys aren't getting cold air; this filter is super dirty. I would say it's well past its change date by months!"

Derrick changed the filter.

"Yeah that seems to fix the problem.... almost immediately I can feel the cold air.", said Derrick.

"Issue solved. It's good to go, let's get out of here bro."

Derrick acted like he didn't hear me; he was too busy trying to pull an R-Kelly. I let his ass be, throwing shade on my way out.

"That's why you ugly and I hope you don't get it."

He laughed.

"Oh, and by the way, yo laugh sound like you're having an asthma attack. You do know them young ones lie about their age, so enjoy prison, I'm gone!"

DERRICK

After I finished shooting my shot with the young thot in the complex, I called Amber back.

"Hey, am I meeting you at the store or the house?"

"The house. Let's wait until traffic dies down. Don't worry I know it's man crush Monday, so you and Jazz just have to hang out."

"Sounds like someone is jealous to me."

"I'm not jealous, you and your boyfriend go have fun."

"Oh, now we gay? It's okay one day were going to find you some friends."

"Nope I'm good, I'm going to be in my bed binge watching *Dangerous Love* until I fall asleep. -- And I do have friends for your information."

"Coworkers don't count boo…"

"Okay bye! bye!"

She always hung up whenever I told the truth. Moments later I pulled up to the house catching Amber and Ashley off guard on their phone and tablet, I honked to scare them. When I got into her car. She looked at me seriously.

"Why would you do that asshole?"

"Because y'all need to be more aware of y'all surroundings. Anyone could walk up on y'all."

"Whatever. That's what this mace is for. You should be happy daycare security didn't mace you for putting your hands on them."

"It was one person."

"You got lucky that one person didn't press charges. They're investigating it as a serious matter. Now the man is on leave of absence and they want us to take Ashley in for a comprehensive physical at their expense to help with the conclusion of this stupid stuff..."

"Why does it have to be stupid? You don't believe what our daughter told me?"

"No, because I talked to her on the way here and she told me that they always play, and he sometimes gives her candy. Not once did she say he touched her in any way. So now my question to you would be, what did you ask her? And what did she say that made you think he was messing with our daughter inappropriately?"

"I don't remember but why would my baby not want to go in?"

I looked at Ashley.

"What did you tell me this morning babe?"

She smiled with her hands coving her face.

"Aw yeah you played daddy?"

"Yea she played you alright, like a game on her tablet.

She always pulls the *I don't wanna go to daycare* or *my head hurts* card. You would be the only one falling for it, now we have to go through all this and that poor guy..."

"Man, I'm sure he's getting paid. It's basically a paid vacation, if anything I did him a favor."

"I hope that you feel bad enough to apologize when you find out that you just made a jackass of yourself."

"Apologize to who? If anything, I fixed his life. I probably scared him straight. Get it? Scared him straight!" I laughed hysterically to myself oblivious to the consequences of my premature actions.

She got out the car rolling her eyes.

"You're so not funny. I just want you to know that."

"I know, I'm hilarious."

She laughed a little bit, like I knew she wanted too.

"No not at all, you better come on before you don't get to see your boo thang tonight."

"Who? That thing in-between your legs? Oh, I never get to see that boo anyway."

"Whatever, I been thinking… We should see a therapist. Maybe a marriage counselor or something, just to strengthen our marriage. I heard my boss talking about how her and her husband sought help and the wonders it has done for them."

I put Ashley in the basket, before trying to kill that idea.

"We don't need no help boo, we all we got, we just need to have more sex and create more of these light skin babies."

"Stop playing Derrick I'm serious!"

"If I say okay, can I get some pooh-nanny?"

"You can get some nanny and some Becky, if you play your cards right."

"Well hell, in that case, what are we waiting for?"

"Okay I'm going to set it up, don't be playing..."

I'D RATHER BE WITH YOU

Despite our issues and the drama today, we were on good terms for the first time in a while. We were laughing and actually talking like adults, instead of screaming at each other, for once. An alert from my phone caught us both off guard. I played it off.

"What's up boo? Keep talking..." I lingered.

"Naw, handle your business, Mr. businessman. It's probably Jazz waiting on his boo." she joked confidently.

I slowed my pace to fall behind Amber and Ashley, I quickly checked the text. It read, "**I'm Pregnant**" from an unfamiliar number. I almost shitted on myself. I wasn't sure who it was but knew I had been hoe-ish enough for it to be a strong possibility. I read it again like the text was going to change.

"Hey babe, I'm going to the bathroom, be right back."

"Okay, we'll be looking for that ice cream you never brought home."

"You know what, you're right. My bad boo, get the biggest one you can find on me."

"You mean on your food stamp connect."

I yelled playfully, "Same thang! I did pay for the connect." I walked away and responded to the text,

"Congratulations and good luck! I'm sure you'll make a great single parent!"

The mystery person sent a sad emoji and responded,

"It's a boy too, how awful for you to say, because I know how bad you want a boy and I know that you didn't have a father growing up."

I responded,

"Yeah, not having a father is a family tradition, every boy has to figure it out on his own. He will grow up stronger than ever. Y'all got this, tell him I love him and best of luck to the both of you."

The mystery person responded,

"Wow Ross, I'm disappointed in you."

There was only one person who called me by my last name like that, and I would never deny her child. I replied,

"I'm just playing love!"

"This is Asia, how are you doing big head?"

"I know exactly who you are now, I admit you had me going at first. Now that I know who my baby mama would be it's all good, I'm excited when is our baby due?"

"Never I'm not having any kids. Ever!"

Now I was the one sending sad emojis. I had been loving this girl since we were kids, it's crazy how life took us on two different paths.

"Hey, I need your help."

"What's up?"

"I bought a tv and it's way too heavy for me to lift by myself, I couldn't even get it out of my trunk."

I got super happy.

"Yeah of course I will help you".

I was excited just to know I was going to see her. It had been so long since we've seen one another.

"Send me the address and I'll be there in like thirty minutes."

I saw Amber from a distance lingering around the clothing isle. I tried to rush her out the store and of course she took notice to it.

"Derrick! You will get to the stupid lounge. It's still early anyway!"

"Jazz said he's trying to leave early because he has to work, that's all."

"Okay well let's go... I'll have to come shopping by myself because y'all are irritating."

"Babe just get what you need. It's no rush. I'm just communicating with you that's all."

"No, we can go. I don't need to spend any money until I get paid anyway."

We stood in line for what seemed like forever and a fucking day. All because the lady in front of us got the wrong apple juice for her WIC voucher. We had a basket full ourselves, the people behind us sighed loudly, obviously frustrated.

"What's the pin again?"

"I thought you had it, you picked up the card, you didn't get it?"

She turned towards me with a lost look. I tried to call Jazz but got no answer.

"Hold on I may still have it in our text from last time."

"You got it?" she rushed.

"Hold on, let me look woman dang!"

"Can I have candy daddy?"

"Baby hold on please..."

"Okay here, I got it, go ahead get what you want boo."

The people behind us looked hella bothered but we didn't give a damn. We had our groceries on top of the free cases of water I normally put under the basket. On our way out, Amber's friendly eyes caught the attention of what I considered unwanted company.

"Oh hey, look it's First Lady!"

"Amber please just keep going and don't say anything."

"That's rude Derrick. They're right there, I'm sure they see us."

First Lady stood with a familiar face. She came over and exchanged hugs with the both of us.

"Hey guys! Good to see you, this is my good friend."

Amber cut her off, "Yes we are familiar."

Ms. Lori filled in the gap. "Yeah I'm Derrick's boss."

"That she is...", I said. First Lady looked shocked and fine as can be in that sundress. I could almost guarantee she wasn't wearing panties. It would be nice if I could bend that ass over in the produce aisle right by the grapes. *--I would tear that ass up.* I thought to myself.

"Wow such a small world huh?", First lady said.

"That's for sure,", said Ms. Lori.

"So, will I see you both this Sunday?"

Amber and her big mouth made plans that I had no intentions on fulfilling.

"Yes ma'am, we will be there!"

"Okay great! I won't keep you guys, I look forward to seeing you both then, take care."

"See you at work Derrick, bright and early!"

"Nope, I'm off. Remember?"

"Oh, that's right. I'm so sorry, you enjoy!"

We went our separate ways.

"Well that was hella weird, and why the hell did you tell her we are going to be at church? I was trying to chill the hole weekend."

"Well looks like your plans have changed huh?"

My phone went off.

"Are you still coming?"

"Dang he's blowing you up isn't he!"

"You know how he gets boo. He's super impatient, he'll be alright."

She had no idea it was really her competition that I never mentioned from years ago.

I made sure my girls were straight, before looking up Asia's address with gps. All this time she lived in the same area, literally eight minutes away. When I got there, she was sitting on the stairs of her complex in her army attire.

"Hey boo!…"

"God it took you long enough! I was just about to ask my creepy neighbor, sheesh."

"Sorry I had to get my baby girl some food."

"It's coo"

"So, I'm assuming it's that big ass box sticking out of your trunk huh?"

"Yeah it's heavy too."

We got it out together, then I tried to be superman just to impress her.

"Here. I'll carry it up, you just open the door."

We walked up the first flight of stairs and it quickly became a work-out.

"Damn what floor you live on?"

"The top."

"Black people always wanna be at the top of something, you do know that's the worst place to be right?"

"How so?"

I was damn near out of breath, I didn't respond until we got to her apartment. I walked around looking through her place trying to conceal my heavy ass breathing.

"Your place is a nice, but the top is the most unstable. I mean where will you go in the case of a tornado?"

"In the tub, where will they go at the bottom if there's a flood?"

"What happens when you're ready to move?"

"I'll call you and the creepy neighbor"

"No, you'll have to ask the creepy dude if he has a brother to help him."

"Aw! So, you wouldn't help me Ross!?"

"I see you still like calling me by the name we should be sharing right now."

"Yep! Too bad you already gave it away..."

"Heyyy, don't do that. I waited a long time for you and you never came."

"That wasn't my fault though Ross, we were kids back then."

"Yeah, I know, but I still felt some type of way."

I started setting up the tv while she changed into sweats and a spaghetti strap shirt.

"Can you bring the other tv off the fireplace in my room?"

It seemed like a trap that I would easily fall for. I didn't realize how big her booty had gotten until I followed her to the back bedroom. It was like my eyes had a slow-motion zoom filter and I watched intriguingly as it wobbled with every step. I wanted her so bad my dick started to slobber. I set the tv on the dresser, it was taking everything in me not to be direct. I was more than willing to grab her up and suck on her pierced nipples that smiled at me through her shirt. My mind was stranded, wondering if her areolas were light, medium, or dark chocolate. Unfortunately, my love for her outweighed the risk. I had a regrettable moment, wishing I would have devoured her hairy, wet lady slower and longer the one opportunity I did get when we were kids, I still stored the taste of her. She was the reason faith was not with me, I had prayed hard and often just to spend my life with her and was never heard, that's when I discovered there was no higher power, we just existed.

"You're all set superstar."

"Aww thank you so much Ross. I owe you dinner or something."

"You don't owe me anything. -- Okay well maybe that baby we discussed in eighth grade."

"Well, when you become unmarried maybe..."

"Hey, I thought you weren't having kids, don't sell me dreams, have my ass looking out the window waiting, then you never show up like my daddy."

She laughed hard as fuck.

"Oh whatever."

"You're lucky I have to go. I'm supposed to meet Jazz tonight."

"Aw really? What has he been up to?"

"Oh nothing... you know he got two girls now?"

"Shut up! Really?!"

"Yep!"

"Well look at both of y'all! All grown up with kiddos."

She walked me to the door. I gave her the longest hug I could afford to get away with.

"I'll see you later beautiful."

"Okay, be safe Ross."

"Goodnight Superstar."

BROTHER FROM
ANOTHER MOTHER

I finally met up with Jazz at Rookie's Lounge.

"What's good bro! You get that good good rest in?"

"For the most part, until your wife came knocking like the police..."

"Yea that sounds like her dramatic ass! Did Ashley do okay for you?"

"Yeah you know she don't give uncle Jazz no problems. I gave her to the girls and let them do they thang. She was complaining that her head hurt, so she ended up sleeping for most of the day."

"Yea she'll be alright, probably not enough sleep.

Damn! I forgot to grab yo card."

"It's all good I'll get it later. You ready to get whooped in some pool?"

"Say no more. Aye guess who I saw just now though?"

"Who?"

"Asia."

"Aw yeah?"

"Man, she still nice looking as always, her booty got phat bruh."

"That's why you late huh?... did you at least tag her?"

"Man, I wish, but you know how that go."

"Aw you went soft. I don't know why you procrastinating, you been liking her since birth."

We laughed.

"Aye you ain't never lied. I still can't believe you messed around with her knowing how your boy felt, but it's all good.... Get to racking!"

"Fool that's old, I told you my fault......I won the last time we were here, so you get to racking!"

"Yeah okay, make sure you call all shots too I know how you like to do."

"Hush dat noise... I got you a beer over there on the table. Aye let me ask you something tho..."

"Only if you make this shot…"

"Bet... uhn -- now answer this for me what is considered cheating to you?"

"It depends, for a man or woman?"

"For both in any order."

"Okay well let me break it down, for us it's when the act actually occurs. For women, it's when they first look at a nigga.

"My Ace! I tried to tell Tosha that same shit."

"You know you can't tell a woman nothing, they don't understand that men are natural flirts and we know how to check ourselves. We tell every bitch the same lie just to see who bite, have them all into us with no real purpose but to make them feel special until we get what we came for and nothing more. Now women, they see a man and just see something new, then start to indulge in a factitious vision wondering what it would be like with him. Not knowing he's playing the same game as her current dude."

"That's crazy because it's like a cycle, we all just messing with each other's woman."

"Yea, pretty much.... Everyone is new to someone, it's the equivalent to thrift store shopping."

"See that's why I don't mind the big girls, y'all sleep on them."

"Who? Not me, they be the wettest! And they give the

best head, jaws be all warm like they pre-heated they mouth for the dick. I'm telling you those are the ones that you have to be careful with. Big girls will fuck yo life up!"

"Oh, I know. But now days these hoes so stuck up, I'm telling you bruh, since Rob died my shit been dry as fuck. One thing I can say he always came through with the hoes."

"He did have some baddies. But bro it's all in your approach, most of them just want to feel special. Get on the net, them social media sites is where it's at. I'm talking about straight past the introduction right into fucking. Most of the women on there be on the same shit we on, and just want to fuck like us. You just have to make them feel comfortable. You have to get personal with them and act like you care about their feelings. I'm telling you, when it's all said and done, y'all both just trying to get a nut, pretend like that makes them experienced and not hoes."

"So, you telling me, that you don't see them as hoes if they just out here smashing niggas racking up their body count because they like dick?"

"Nigga you not even listening! Hell to the fuck yes that makes them hoes! I said pretend, key word pretend! Me personally I believe in polygamy."

CHEAT CODE

"Jazz what have I always said? You remember?"

"Of course..."

"Then what I say?"

"You said if her tv is a 32-inch, sitting on milk crates or a family dollar tv stand, then you automatically smashing. And if I see an xbox or play station game system, a nigga lives there, he's just locked up."

"Damn right and don't ever forget it!"

He busted out laughing along with the ease dropping bartender.

JAZZ

"But all jokes aside, I think Tosha is messing around with someone..."

Derrick immediately got pissed off as if it was his situation.

"Say what bruh, what makes you think that?"

"Clues big dog, you know the tell-tell signs."

"You have to be more specific!"

"So, you know Tosha is a home body, right? Well lately she been overdoing it with the makeup and going out just about every weekend. A few times she came home all sloppy looking like she just got done riding the D. She's starting to wear panties I've never seen before. They gotta be new, it be them sexy joints too, you know the ones that motivate you to give them head. Plus, her ass be all happy and shit for no reason, singing stupid ass Keyshia Cole and K. Michelle songs all extra loud, like she trying to hint something. I caught her smiling at her phone while texting a few times. Those clues nigga....and guess what?"

"What?", said Derrick.

"One night I went outside to grab something out of the car, and noticed that her passenger seat was leaned back, I'm talking about way back!"

"Aw, well, damn, yeah it's definitely something going on. But then again it could be nothing, you probably just tripping bro, but, so...I mean, what's up, shoot me straight, when did you first notice she was moving different?"

"I'm going to be one hundred with you."

"That's what homies should do."

"Remember my birthday weekend when you, Terry, and I went to Club Pure and I was hella fuc..."

He cut me off.

"-- Bro don't feed me the sympathy intro, you know I remember, so what's up?"

"Okay so look, I was telling Tosha for the longest that I wanted to have a threesome one day."

"As we all do.... I'm following. Keep going."

"Well she came through for a nigga that night, when y'all dropped me off Tosha was at the damn door soon as I got in. She covered my eyes and walked me to our room where she had another chick waiting. We did every position, it was as if they were running a train on me, more than it was a threesome. Keep in mind the whole time it was dark and they we're doing most of the positioning. I didn't do no work my dude, yet they still made it burp like a baby three times, best night ever ya dig."

"Hell yeah, I would say. Okay so, what's the problem?

Sounds like you're a spoiled spouse complaining at this point."

"I'm sure it does but listen to this, you know how you can tell who is who? Like you know Amber well enough to know when it's not her right?"

"Yeah of course."

"Well I could tell that it wasn't Tosha who was topping me off, because she was out-performing my wife dog. I mean, yeah, I was drunk but I know my wife not that good, if it were a contest, I would have to judge it ten to two honestly. I never cum off head and that's how I got the first one off. She was cleaning me out too, her hand motion game was decent like tug of war, and her mouth produced foam, not spit nigga. Foam! I mean large puddles hitting my feet with every tug."

"What was Tosha doing while ol girl was putting in work?"

"This was in the beginning, she must have just been watching but like I said, it was kinda weird at first because not once did they interact with each other. It was just me touching both of them, like one was riding my dick and the other was riding my face, then they would switch. Now guess what?"

"Dude what?"

"I found out that it was her fucking mama dog!"

"Whoa, wait! What...?!Woooww! Oohh shit, you smashed fine ass Ms. Gwen?! Kudos, but DAMN, and Tosha set this up?"

"Yes, it was all her bruh."

"Wow. Aw man, that's major, I'm next nigga set that shit up! You laughing like I'm playing. I'm kinda jealous to be honest, I mean not that I would want to fuck my in-law, ugh. But nigga your mother-in law is fine. She doesn't look her age at all, black don't crack baby. So, what's the problem though? And how did you find out it was her mama? Tosha?"

"That's where I'm going with this, Tosha never said anything. There was no problem until I found out it was her mama. One day her mama was watching the kids while Tosha and I got some alone time in. That next morning, I woke up early to go get the kids and of course they asses sleep hard and wakeup midday like they work a night shift job or something. But anyway, I get there about to wake them up and Gwen asked if I could check her cable source because she couldn't get it on the right input in her room. So, me being the good son-in-law that I am, I go check it out. Next thing I know she came up behind me and went straight for the bull horn. I tried my best not to get hard, mind you it's early in the morning so naturally it's ready at the peak of daylight. I'm like, *"hold up what's going on Ms. Gwen what are you doing honey"* ...she's like, *"it's nothing I haven't felt before"*, I was still lost backing my way up to the door. She pushes it closed and backs me up against the wall next to it. Before I knew it, she was putting in manual labor with her mouth, it was then that I realized *"--oh shit--"* it was her in the room that night. It was the same unmistaken overflow of head."

"Bro you're selfish! You couldn't call me? As many times as I shared with you, I'm curious now, you making it sound all good! You know what, just because I'm openly jealous I'm going to be a hater and call you a nasty ass dude, getting head from your fine ass mother-in-law! Who does that?! It should have been me and I bet she got you off again huh?"

"Naw, she almost got it tho'. My youngest Jayla came busting through the door! I guess her nana wasn't smart enough to think about locking the door. She definitely planned that out, and you know Jayla told her mama something, we been off since then."

"Well I mean you can't be upset with Tosha; you're messing with her mama dog!"

"But she brought that our way not me, this is mostly

her fault. Now she wants to be a hoe out here."

"Nigga man up, that doesn't make her a hoe just because she picked up the other controller and put the game on two players. Sometimes the tables turn, you know that...... just give her some space J."

"Damn why it feel like you are taking up for her, you my boy remember."

"Calm yo sensitive ass down, I'm not taking up for no one. You like a brother to me, been knowing you forever and a day. Once you married her, she became like a sister to me. You can't be in an uproar about it. Remember you got away with some pretty fucked up shit Jazz, like that time you laid up with ol girl and brought bedbugs home. Tosha endured some crazy mess with you too, right now the shoe on the other foot, we both know if you leave your door unlocked somebody is bound to walk in. There's no point in you investigating who it is. It's probably best that your crazy ass doesn't know. Number one rule.... If a man smashes your chick..."

"Blame yo woman not his dick......yeah, yeah, I know, I still feel some type of way."

"Of course, you're going to, you're supposed to, that's like someone repossessing your car. But know this, you can't be out here chasing. Just let her do her for a minute...

she will come back they always do... Plus there isn't shit out here but a bunch of niggas who wanna fuck. She's a married woman, there is nothing they can do but entertain her ass, she'll be back."

"Yea hopefully, got me over here losing sleep barely eating and shit."

He tried to cheer me up.

"Aye you remember when we were in Issac's basement smoking that kush and this foo Issac told you that you couldn't put your pop on the coffee table? You asked, *"why not"*, then he said, *"because it's for coffee!"* ..."

We busted out laughing.

"Yea I remember, I don't see how you work with that dude on a daily, he dumb as hell. Aye I'm going to take your advice on this one and fall back, but if the shit goes too far left, I have to throw the flag bruh. I can't keep letting her slide, this isn't a playground."

DERRICK

"Alright bro" I said trying to end the conversation. I didn't have any more advice to dish out, but it seemed like the situation was about to get serious real fast. I had to do something. I had to make sure it didn't spiral out of control, suddenly, my phone went off.

"Oh shoot! At least somebody got some action who's that?", Jazz said.

"Aw, nobody important. Just this little chick I met at the gas station."

"You stay with one, I'm not mad at it. Well, bro I gotta hit this clock, I'll catch up with you. Aye be safe, text me that address if you ride out."

"Will do big dog."

I got so wrapped up in our conversation I almost forgot to text back.

"Aye we need to link up, let me know when you're free."

She replied with an address and a room number saying,

"Meet me here now!"

CROSSING LINES

It led me to a casino where she checked into a master suite with multiple rooms, she purposely left the swing bar in the door so it would remain cracked. It was safe to say she was expecting me. I heard the shower running from the open space where I was about to have a seat until she opened the steam filled bathroom. She stood in the doorway naked, lavished up in soap pointing at me to come here.

TOSHA

Once he got close enough, I pulled him into the double pane glass shower, clothes on and all. He sucked on my nipples before lifting my body in the air with my back against the wall. My legs hung over his shoulders crossing together once he spread my pussy apart exposing my pretty girl. He grabbed the spray nozzle shooting my pussy at close range with the beaded water, then galloping his tongue in a sequence multiple times, at various levels until my clit swelled. I thought for sure his mouth had grown tired once he brought me down, but he surprised me when he went to his knees facing me against the wall under the shower head. He stuck his whole face in my thirty-two-inch ass, eating like he was starving. The side of my face along with my hands pressed against the slippery wall of tile. The water blessed my spine running down the crease of my gutter, enhancing the feeling where he was working.

"Ouuu damn..."

He was doing his thing. With nothing to grip, I soon made fist of my shaky hands. I was trying to stay strong for my legs that wanted to buckle once he put his fingers inside my pussy, mixing and mastering the art of satisfaction. His rich tongue delivered joy to my brown sugar alley with every unique strobe he made. I couldn't take it anymore. Using my hand to pry his head away from my ass hole, I turned the water off. He looked at me like he was a dog and I had taken his food.

"What... why are you looking like that?"

"Why did you stop me like that?"

"Because you know what you're doing, and I didn't know what my body was about to do if you get my drift. Here take your clothes off, I have some more towels in the room."

He sat his muscled backside in the room chair by the vent air drying his nicely shaved manhood by the window unit as I lotioned up. I grabbed my wireless ear buds and crawled in between his legs, he maneuvered his hands through my hair while I squeezed his stiffness and searched for a good jaw work out playlist. I was under for close to an hour giving him my best stroke jacking it off with two hands, providing that twisting motion that I saw my mama using. It must have worked because I felt his toes curling beside my knees.

He grabbed my chin leaning in to kiss me in the mouth. I sat on his lap riding several laps, that's when he took control raising up while still inside of me, he bent me over the bed spreading my ass cheeks to slide his finger inside my glory hole while pulling my hair with his free hand.

"Aw yeah, you like this dick?"

My mouth was pinned opened like I was deaf learning how to talk. He was hard and thick. I looked back and saw him looking down admiring his dick coast in and out.

"Oh my, right there. Yes, ouu yes."

He was fucking me like a trophy was involved, he pulled out, turning me over, smacking his dick against my clit.

"Whew shit that pussy good."

"Why you are teasing me baby?", I said

I grabbed it, sticking it back inside of me. We created echo claps each time our skin met. He had one of my legs over his shoulder while sucking on my toes, hitting it harder before going into a fourth position rotating me to the side. He propped my left knee up to my stomach guiding his curved dick in my tunnel nice and easy. I felt my pussy tighten up. He lifted my arched knee higher, fucking me in a slope. I gripped the sheets and smothered my face down in the pillow to

suppress my moans. He was being generous with his stroke until I put my hand up pressing against his stomach trying to keep him from going too deep. He clamped down on my wrists.

"Nah don't run, you better take this dick, I want all this pussy!"

"Ohh damn, fuuucck!"

"Who's is it!?"

"Yours ouhh shit it's yours baby!"

He was fucking the feeling out of my pink cookie, I felt the promise of a successful build up within.

"Oooo yes don't stop I'm about to..."

DERRICK

My ass cheeks locked in, I caught a cramp in my leg, in the same moment the door swung open. My dick instantly turned into a gummy. Tosha jumped up grabbing the sheets to cover her body, I ducked peaking over the edge of the bed.

My adrenaline was pumping, there was silence for a brief second.

"Mama?" Jayla called out in curiosity.

Tosha replied in a ghetto ass tone.

"Jayla... What the hell are you doing out of bed?"

"I heard some noises mama, I got scared."

They carried on a childlike conversation.

"It's ok baby, it was nothing... go back in the other room and lay down. I'll come check on you in a second."

Jayla's little interfering ass walked out leisurely.

Tosha rushed to the door, closing it softly.

"Are you ready to finish me off?"

I was scrambling around the room forgetting my clothes were in the shower wet.

"You didn't tell me you had the girls here, that would have been nice to know!"

"First off, I only have one of the girls here, only

because my baby didn't have anywhere to go, and Nia is going to school from her friend's house tomorrow. How could you not know I had at least one kid with me? You see I have a suite. I'm just going to get a two-bedroom suite for myself?"

"Hell, you could have had your mama in here with you I don't know."

"Now why would I have... Ooh you talked to Jazz huh? He told you the story, didn't he?"

"I mean we talked but..."

"Yeah, he told you, I know he did!"

"Okay yeah, he told me, and my dude is losing his mind."

"What do you think he's going to lose when he finds out what we've been doing for the past seven months?"

"Aw him finding out about this is not even an option... that's why I'm here, we gotta cut this off, this shit is foul."

"Oh, and you just came to that conclusion after all this time, plus what we just did?"

"I'm just saying Tosh, we did our thang, we had our fun. Sometimes it's best to go out on top. If we get too greedy this could get ugly fast."

"Well, let it get ugly! I enjoy what we do, I'm sure he's out here doing him. Not to mention messing with my mama!"

"But Tosha you introduced that world to him…"

"It was a one-time thing… I was trying to do something special for his punk ass."

"Still you can't fault him, he said he never knew it was your mother that night and she came onto him when he went to get the kids."

"Well his dick should have never got hard, that's on him!"

"Come on Tosha, be fair here. We're talking about your fine ass mama. I can't lie, hell my dick would have gotten hard too."

"Umm"

"What? I'm just speaking facts."

"So, what we have going on is over? Is that what you're saying?"

"I mean you are my best friend's wife. How long do you think this can continue without us getting caught?"

"As long as we want it to."

"You know the universe doesn't work like that; karma always find its way back. Just know that I enjoyed our time and we have the best secret to keep. Take everything we did and store it within your memory, you can always close your eyes and imagine who you want while having sex. I do it all the time with Amber."

"Aw yeah who do you think of?"

"You, duh!"

"Yeah don't play me for a dumb bitch."

"I'm for real, it be like that sometimes."

"Yeah let me find out your out here giving it away!...
Okay okay, I guess the hoe in me understands what you're
saying. Can we do it one more time?"

"Girl it's close to morning!"

"My point, you might as well stay the rest of the
morning so I can get another nut out of you. Let's start our
day off right."

I went along with it, handling business quickly, I
stuffed her with dick while peeking my thumb in and out
her backdoor. Once I felt my debt was served, I went home
to wash her scent off me before sliding in bed behind
Amber's soft, warm body.

AMBER

I woke up early that morning with a gut feeling that was screaming at me, I just knew Derrick was up to no good. Like always I couldn't prove anything, I had no evidence, but I knew something wasn't right. He smelled like Irish spring. And on top of that, he woke in a cold sweat searching for the phone that I had been trying to sneak from under his big ass head for the past thirty minutes.

WOMAN'S INTUITION

My suspicion only enhanced from his suspect behavior.

"Babe where you put my phone?"

That comment alone made me want to hit him in his damn face. I knew it was his way of seeing if I tampered with it.

"It's under your pillow where you always hide it, remember?"

"Dang why the attitude! You always tripping. Nobody is trying to hide anything! It's five in the morning and you at it already on that power trip. You were just hella coo yesterday."

"Boy please, I wake up happy and positive every day.

I'm not worried about you, take your ass back to sleep! I'm going to the gym."

"That's your problem right there, you're angry at me because you don't get enough sleep, and as my wife you should worry about me. Like damn, can a nigga get a kiss instead of an attitude for a change."

"Can a nigga brush his teeth and wash his face first, then maybe you can get some love. Why don't you try getting up and being on time to work for a change? Maybe you will feel good about yourself, I don't know how you still have a job."

"I feel good getting my complete ten hours of sleep, who in their right mind says --*hey I'm going to get up earlier than I should, just to do the same shit I did yesterday again today.*"

"First of all, you're an idiot, Derrick! It's eight hours not ten, since you know everything what does listen mean?"

"Can you sound it out please?"

"You know what, I don't have time to go back and forth with you. I should have been at the gym by now getting these squats in."

"Aww you must be trying to keep that ass right for your side nigga" I said feeling guilty.

"I'm trying to keep it tight for you, but you can't even act right."

"What are you talking about?"

"It doesn't matter I'm out. I'll be back to get Ash make sure she's ready.".

Before he could say a word to piss me off, I bounced feeling distracted by his ladder of lies. I just wanted to hit the tread meal and see some eye candy. I stopped at the fast mart for a bottle water and some yogurt. The yogurt was a bonus, I mainly stop for the water and the attention I get from the down to earth white guy with the hood personality and dope haircut. I typically didn't take interest in white men, young white men at that, but it's something about the way he looks at me with that baby face and those light, avocado green eyes.

He could get it, if I wasn't married…. man. I won't lie I get a bit of a tingle feeling in my pants when he speaks. His breath is always pleasant, it's such a turn on, a man with good breath, *yes lord!* I almost have to remind myself that I am married. *--Jesus be a fence!* … I was ready to trade it all, but I knew it was just the thought of something new that intrigued me.

I kept it pushing giving my best invitation to imaginary possibilities with a smile on my way out the door. I got about an hour of gym time in before calling it quits. Anna at the front desk tried talking me into signing up for yoga classes. I was tempted but declined the offer.

"You would have fun in there Amber!"

"Umm na girl that's way too odd for me. I feel like the men pretend to be interested in the class just come to see females in weird positions. They would be getting just what they came for, staring at the white girl with the vixen booty, I'll pass.

"You're so funny." She said.

"I'm serious! Even the gay ones turn back curious sometimes!"

"I understand, I know how they can be."

"Exactly! I'll see you tomorrow Anna."

I headed back home feeding my spirit with positive vibes and gospel music along the way. When I made it to the house Derrick was in the bathroom and I'll be damn, I finally caught him slipping. His phone was sitting naked on the dresser, it was almost too good to be true. This was nobody but God telling me something, because his phone is always glued to him. Regardless of what he's doing weather it's showering, shitting or shaving you better believe it's nearby. I hurried to see what I could find, and it didn't take long. Before I could even unlock it there was a message from an unidentified number. He was smart enough to have a fingerprint lock but dumb enough to have the same password as our daughter's birthday. Once I clicked on the message a picture of some random woman exposed popped up with the caption:

"It's ready for you."

My blood was boiling but I stayed collected. I calmly took my phone off my armband to snap proof of the fuckery and the chick's number. I knew he was going to lie about it. I couldn't wait to see what his ass had to say about this foul play. I tried to be quick enough to find more dirt but heard the bathroom door open. I pressed the power button to sleep the phone and went about undressing.

"Dang babe you almost scared the mess out of me, when did you get here?"

I knew I couldn't let the cat out of the bag yet, so I played it coo.

"Just now, what time did you get in last night? I woke up at two and you still weren't here, you were out late all last week too."

"Yeah boo after Jazz and I left, Russell called and asked me to help him clean the caves. I'm trying to help us get ahead and pay some of these bills down. Why, what's up is something wrong?"

"Naw babe, I was just asking, get your money. Okay I'm out, I can't afford to be late today. We have all these meetings in place for the new plus procedures, so I won't be able to call and wake you up or be on the phone like that because the new supervisor is a real bitch."

I really just didn't want to be bothered with Derrick's ass today.

"Okay it's all good boo, I'm up anyway. Try to have a good day"

If he only knew it was too late for that. As quick as he leaned in for a kiss, I turned to the side.

"Here you go with that…"

I tried my best to keep my emotions in check, but I wouldn't be me if I didn't hit him with a hint, that I was no dummy.

"I don't know where your lips been." He looked at me with the, damn she knows something face, then acted like I was crazy.

"What, where did that come from?

"Nowhere…"

Ashley walked in the room.

"Hey pooh, you're up just in time. Daddy's going to spend his whole day with you!" He hugged Ashley and said some words that I didn't catch, my only concern was making sure he knew, that I knew something.

Women Be Like...

I couldn't wait to get to work just to take my mind off all the bs I was dealing with at home. Work was normally my escape place, and today was no different. I walked into Brittany screaming...

"Ayyyyee! It's my birthday month bitch!"

"What, birthday month?! Child please you get one day of birth like the rest of us, maybe two, because I can almost believe it took at least two days to push out your big ass head, but it didn't take your mother a whole damn month to have you." joked Mike.

"Stop hating Mike!"

That's all it took for an interesting exchange between a group of my drama filled coworkers to erupt. Mike was always being messy, starting conversations by making controversial statements that he knew dang well these black women would be defensive about.

"Females with government assistance always want houses with big ass yards then want someone to cut it!"

Danielle said, "Damn Mike! That's how you feeling? How we go from her birthday to that? And if that's the case, I believe if a man is getting any of a woman's cookie it shouldn't be a problem. Any man who's reaping a woman's benefits should be able to cut the grass, cook, clean, fix a leak or something, nothing is free!

Mike countered, "That's prostitution then, am I right or wrong?"

Ree Ree jumped in like it was a tag team.

"Boy bye, that's compensation. What I don't get is how a woman could allow a man to stick his worm inside her and get nothing out the deal. Now me, honey when I tell you I'm getting all mine, trust me, because my light bill be the same as my raggedy ass check sometimes. Makes me wonder if the light company doing our payroll too. Therefore, if I put this wet muscle on any man, I'm securing the bag. Hell, nine times out of ten we don't get to cum and y'all nut before we can even get our imagination together to think about the man we really want to be humping."

By this time, I had to put my two cents in.

"You guys want us to have all these damn dick sucking skills. *Do it like this, do it like that, put more spit on it, put it all the way in your throat and hum.* So, hell yeah, he better have some type of skills."

Stacy bisexual ass looked at me crazy.

"Dang girl, you mad or naw? You a freak though if you are doing all that, what's your number?" she joked.

"Yeah okay my husband not going for that, I'm just saying they expect too much for too little, can't even keep a bitch happy mentally these days."

"Fuck that! Just make sure your sucking dick with your eyes open, niggas be recording.," Angie said.

Ree Ree said, "Girl you are so random."

"I'm just saying I had a nigga put me out there before, all on the net, but lucky for me I sucked that bone so good it backfired in my favor. I got hell of likes and followers off that video."

Then Shawn or Shawndrica, as he or she now likes to be called, voiced her crazy ass opinion.

"It sounds like someone is cheating to me, you know what they say, I'm not sucking dick spelled backwards is your homegirl will."

Everyone got quite as hell looking at me all awkward, I tried to retreat.

"He's just more flirtatious than I'd like for him to be, but that's most men right..."

Ree Ree said, "That's true, but either way men are never satisfied with one woman, even when they put that commitment ring on and give you their dumb last name. My grandma used to have guys over all the time while my grandpa was at work and she'd always tell my sisters and I that they were our uncles. Eventually we got old enough and smart enough to realize what was going on. One day my sister mustered up the courage to ask our grandma why she was playing grandpa like that. And Grandma said, *"Because Sometimes pa-pa forgets that some games are two players. Remember baby, just because a man marries you, doesn't mean that his eyes stop working, sometimes you have to remind them that yours haven't either."*

Angie said, "Girl yo grandma was just a hoe!"

We all busted out laughing including Ree.

Toya made her way into the conversation as usual. See I can't have some negro stressing me out, messing up my ph balance. That's why I'm getting me a white man and when I decide to get serious, I'm keeping his ass a secret. I'm not telling nobody! Not even my mama. Because she will probably try and fuck him too!"

"Girl you silly!"

"I'm just saying my mama still be out here fucking and if a woman's pussy is functional, she'll fuck a man in her presence if the opportunity presents itself. I know I would if he looks good enough. That's why you can't be out here telling these hoes how happy you are, how much he spoils you, or how good he is in bed. Bitches get curious and start thinking. Like I said I'm not sharing his ass with social media, my mama, hell not even my daddy! His ass might be on some fruity shit too! Oh, and whenever he has unknown numbers calling, I'm answering it like, *new phone who is this...*"

"Seriously, wow y'all are on one today."

The laughs were much needed but short lived once Shawndrica brought up some bull.

"Amber you should have been built you a team, I know for a fact that your man had relations with Tiffany in HR. I used to see him waiting in the parking lot and every time she came out her ass was cheesing. Trust me ain't no female smiling that hard at somebody else's husband for no reason. You need to be like me, fuck him...then get some answers..."

"Girl please that never works."

"I didn't say he was going to give them to you, but when you have that gut feeling he's bound to slip up. All men have two things in common, when they eat, they get sleepy and when they nut, they get sleepy. If he hasn't ate, feed him. Then fuck him and his ass will be under like anesthesia. That's a knockout! You go through that phone, better known as a nigga's diary, and find out how many siblings your baby has."

"Girl you are something special, not siblings."

"I'm serious! Why do you think it's with them all the time? I'm telling you they don't sit it face down for no reason and they don't cut it off for the lame excuse of wanting personal time with no interruptions. You better know a dog is going to be a dog and not one of them is going to volunteer information willingly. It's going to be a lie followed by some commas and a stutter. You fuck him then you get some answers... I'm just saying."

Sandra said, "Girl if you don't get your ass back to that damn cubicle and take some calls with yo crazy behind!"

"No bitch, you need to be humble and stay woke, literally! Act like your sleeping one night when he comes home. If he's creeping all soft, peeking his head around the doorways to see if you're up, honey that's the first clue that he's on some bullshit! If his trifling behind go to the bathroom and put out a long hard piss followed by a nasty ass fart and a sigh of relief, then the water run for a good minute like he thoroughly cleaning in his hands... which we know niggas don't do properly... Ooo bitch trust me when I say, he's washing some shit off his dick! Be smart, sniff his fingertips too because you know that condom smell sticks, or you could get some scissors and cut off a piece of his pubic hair while he's asleep. Make sure you take it from under his balls tho', because that's where the pussy juices roll. Put it in a cap full of peroxide and if it fizzles up... that's how you know for sure he's fucking around! But don't trip because revenge is the best experiment known to woman. Girl go buy you some of that installation they be putting inside the walls of a house and rub that shit all in his socks and underwear! Then invest in a good dildo."

"Amber don't listen to these hoes! We all know life has more side effects than a birth control patch, the key is to never be bitter, be better honey... Keep pushing and don't you dare go waste no money on a dildo! CBCB sis!", Brittany said excitedly.

We all looked dumbfounded at each other.

"Okay maybe I'm being the clueless white girl right now, but what the hell is cbcb?"

"Cucumber, banana, curling iron, brush handle -- all the basic multipurpose dicks I'm sure all you hoes have around the house that can easily replace a sixty-dollar toy. Put a condom on one and live your best life, without getting an overdraft fee or STD."

"Girl what! Umm no, that won't work for me. I need mine to vibrate and stimulate my clit."

"Oh, I have a solution for that too. Get your man's game controller and put in Call of Duty. Put the handle part against your clit and let the online players keep killing you. Oou GIRL! That vibration is something different, it's strong as hell but feels so damn good!

Whew! Y'all sleep..."

"Brittany your taking this saving money shit too far bitch...but I'm listening so what do you recommend for anal?", Ree Ree asked.

"Oh wow, I'm done listening. Y'all are too nasty for me."

Angie chimed in.

"Fuck all that, I just want a good man! He doesn't even need to have a big dick, just thick enough to plug my hole with a credit score past poor..."

"See that's what I'm talking about Angie! Goals girl, goals! I bet it's a man with four solid inches somewhere right now praying to meet a woman like you."

Shawndrica's manly ass added her thought's again...

"Bitch please, a nigga will say whatever to get in your panties but his ass definitely not praying for you."

"Well, I have faith that there are still some great men out here, don't worry about him. He's just hating, keep your head up girl."

GIVE AND TAKE

Later that evening I went home. Derrick wasn't there.

I cleaned the house from top to bottom, poured me some wine, and fixed his favorite meal. I was feeling hella good. Derrick made it in with almost perfect timing. I had just got Ashley settled for bed.

"Why is baby girl yelling her prayers out loud?"

"Because I told her to... so God can hear her."

He laughed.

"Okay then..."

"What's so funny smart ass?"

"Nothing babe, if that's the plan, I respect it."

"What do you mean the plan?"

He played me off, stripping down to his drawls,

getting comfortable. I disciplined myself enough to try a new approach. Rather than creating an argument or having an attitude, I thought I would try some of the suggestions that were brought up in our work conversation. *--Please him first, then feed him.* As stupid as it sounded, I was desperate enough to try anything that would possibly start a positive change in our marriage. I remember Toya saying take the random opportunities to smell his dick which sounded ridiculous, but there is no security in my heart plus they sounded experienced. I had nothing to lose. I met him as he was about to exit the room, I quickly shut the door before he could escape. He must have thought I was on trip mode or something.

"Oh, here you go, what now?"

I caught him by surprise when I grabbed his penis making it a solid matter within seconds.

"Ouuu damn! Who are you and where's my wife?"

I didn't bother to respond to his sarcasm, I was focused on the mission. I eased to my knees pulling his pipe out of his sweats. I purposely left the light on so I could watch his facial expressions in the process. Guess I wasn't discreet enough.

"Aw you have to smell it now before you lick it? That's fucked up!"

Refusing to get distracted, I put my bullet in the palm of my hand at the highest speed and pressed it against his balls. I gripped his dick firmly with my free hand while giving him my best super head impression.

"Damn babe! Yeah just like that, oouu shit"

It felt good knowing I could still please my man, he came faster than normal releasing his offspring on my face. I sucked the rest out of him before it got sensitive and went limp. I knew he was done once he laid across the bed.

"Babe that head reminded me of when we first meet... whew."

It didn't take long before he was out cold, I sat there staring at him knowing that I allowed him to get away with some fucked up stuff, but I loved the mess out of his dirty dick ass.

Once again, I couldn't help but to forgive and forget like it never happened. I took my mind off the negatives by focusing on the positives, somehow my mind drifted thinking about trips we should take. Then I started hearing something. I thought that I was tripping at first but as I got closer to the wall, it became clear that our neighbors were getting it in. I tried not to pay them any attention, but they were noisy as fuck. The louder it got the more I became turned on; their moans were like soft porn to my ears. I looked over at Derrick before putting my ear flush against the wall, deeply invading their privacy. I started playing with myself imagining that it was me in her place. I made it quick so Derrick didn't catch my horny ass doing this shit. He left me hanging so I had to be good to myself. I finished before the chick on the other side of the wall did. Crawling in bed, I rubbed my slimy fingers in Derrick's beard like it was moisturizer. I laid on his chest and fell asleep.

Things were moving smoothly for us the past few months, I decided to keep up the momentum by motivating myself to enroll in next semester classes. I was focused on three goals, family stability, financial security, and pleasing God. I was on a natural high that I didn't want to fall from. Derrick and I were good, life was great, work was the usual work, and the tea was always juicy. In fact, it was so juicy, I needed a spiritual and mental vacation from the messiness. I just wanted to be around positive energy and good vibes for a change. That Wednesday evening after work, I cooked dinner, and left Derrick and Ashley home watching movies while I attended Sisterhood Empowerment at the church.

I was running a little behind but it's always a surprise party when a group of Godly women come together in a small intimate setting.

FULL CIRCLE

I tried to walk in unseen but as soon as I opened the door, some of the ladies just had to look back. *Women will be women*, I guess we're all a little nosy. Their reaction to my entrance created a lack of attention towards First Lady, she paused putting me in the spotlight jokingly.

"Ladies, say hello to Amber..."

Kim put her hand in the air inviting me to join her table. I thought her gesture was odd because normally in church she just gives a strange look and hardly ever speaks. From the time I took a seat she was talking to me as if we were buddy, buddy.

"Hey girl! You made it just in time. We're about to partner up. First Lady is about to walk us through a womanhood exercise."

"Oh really, like a game?"

"Yes."

"Oh okay, that's different from what we often do, I'm ready..."

"Okay ladies, this challenge is called trading places. By a show of hands how many of you have husbands?... Okay not bad... So, most of us in the room know what seeing one person daily from the time you wake until the time you go to sleep, can do to your mental?"

We all laughed.

"That's okay, that's why we come here to get a peace of mind ...right? Hey, I'll be the first to say there has been a few times that you guys were going to be Pastor-less come Sunday morning oookay... I'm just saying now!"

She chuckled hard like there was real-life truth behind that statement.

"I'm joking, well kind of sort of, let's just thank God for delivering me from those thoughts. Amen! In all seriousness, marriage is a blessing. That's why tonight I want to encourage those of you who do not yet have a husband. Until you get one don't play the role of a wife. That means don't give a man all the benefits of a husband to receive the title of girlfriend. Know your worth honey and don't let him lay if he can't stay!"

She looked at one woman directly and said,

"Look at you girl! Now you know you got it going on and should have a husband, but if I were to guess, I would say that you're the reason that you are not a good thing. How many of you ladies caught that?"

A bunch of us looked around the room to make sure that we weren't the only ones who didn't get it. Eventually she broke it down.

"Why you ladies looking lost!? Oh Lord, Iesha put Proverbs 18:22 on the projector, the NIV version please. Now let's all read it together:"

He who finds a wife finds what is good and receives favor from the Lord.

"So, the question I would like each of you to ask yourself, is -- *Am I a good thing*? Now if you can't answer that question with a yes, then most likely you're one of the ones who is not married. And if you're married and can't say yes, maybe you're in one of those dry places in your marriage where you forgot the vows you promised, not only to that man but to God as well. And yes, we can argue the case of he doesn't do this anymore and all the ten thousand other reasons. But understand this, it's not about what he no longer does, it's about you being the kingdom woman God designed you to be... right? It's about the good thing that the bible says you are."

It felt like we were getting personal. Kim leaned over and said to me.

"This is on point."

I couldn't do anything but agree, I had to adjust my seat for this message.

"Now ladies, I know some of you are wondering what does a good thing look like outside of context. Well, you have to refer back to context. You have to read the word. Reading in general is very attractive to a man by the way, thought I'd throw that out there. I'm telling you, it's something about a woman laid up in bed after a nice hot shower with a glass of wine and reading, that intrigues me... I mean a man. See y'all got me getting excited myself trying to give y'all secrets! It's okay, a room full of women can be women... right? I'm telling you... try it one day, one minute you're reading a book, the next your creating the book. But back to this book. The text tells us in Ephesians 5:22: *"Wives submit yourselves to your husbands as to the Lord."* So, the bible is saying, the same way you would submit yourself to God is the same way you should serve your husband and he should serve unto the Lord. Now women hear me out when I say this, he may not serve the Lord as he should, but you hold your own accountability and do your part because ultimately that's how you'll be judged in heaven. We're going to role play a little. I want you to partner up with someone, preferably married women together."

Kim got all excited like she knew what we were about to do, she took it upon herself to name me as her game partner. I much rather would have liked to be with Andrea or someone I was more comfortable with. But of course, I didn't want to come off rude, so I went along with it.

"Okay, so the objective of this game is to find out if you are the best woman that you can be, for the man who chose you to be. I want you to imagine that you have swapped husbands or significant others with the woman in front of you. Gather the backdrop information about each other's life, then take turns explaining how a typical day would be for her husband with you. It's a bit confusing but does everyone have it?"

Collectively we all muttered, "Yes."

Kim insisted that I go first with a big smile on her face. I was starting to feel like I came on the wrong day. I kept it brief and aimed to participate.

"Okay -- well Derrick and I have one daughter as you know. I think a typical day for your husband in my household would be waking up to breakfast on the stove. I would most likely be gone for work so he would take Ashley to daycare and then go to work himself. I would grab food on the way home, normally its pizza, chicken, or chinese... depending on what day it is. The nightcap would consist of me washing clothes while they probably glue themselves to the tv or something. Then I go to sleep."

"Oh wow interesting..."

"What?"

"Oh nothing, I just know my husband wouldn't want to eat out that much, that's all. But a little bit about our lifestyle... I don't work, so he is the main provider. We have no kids and we love to travel. A day in our household for your husband would be like a roller coaster, literally. I would ride him early in the morning then he would eat me for breakfast, which means that we would miss breakfast, but lunch would be special. We would go to our normal spot where we always get this gorgeous Spanish server name Juliana. I would sit beside him in the booth drinking endless mimosa's until Juliana comes over to great us with her sexy accent. I would put my hand in Derrick's pants enlarging his freedom and talk about the fun positions we could do in the bedroom with her."

Right in the middle of her talking, I received a text from Tosha asking if I could call her. I told her I would after I left my social event.

Kim leaned over being nosy, "Who's that? Derrick?"

I didn't even respond, and I sure as hell didn't like the way she said my husband's name as if she knew him like that. It was starting to get to me, and to be honest, I was tired of being social with this chick. Something was off about her and it didn't sit well.

"Okay time is up! Now you ladies have homework. I want you to email me what attracts you the most about your significant other, along with a short-term goal that you would like for your marriage. With that being said.... let's pray so we can get you out of here. Come in close don't be scared, this is a sisterhood! I won't feed it to you, but I want each of you ladies to receive this, *"Lord we come to you with a sound mind. We thank you for the gift of womanhood, the presence of sisterhood. Lord, write it on our hearts to be all that you call us to be for your glory. Lord, if any woman in this room is broken father, we ask for a breakthrough right now! Retire defeat Lord, retire insecurity, and restore confidence in marriage. God, I pray that you guide each of these women home safely as we depart this sanctuary where you have uplifted us tonight. Lord thank you for your word, thank you for your grace and all the ladies say... Amen."*

I hurried to get away from Kim. I now knew not to ever sit by her ass again. I was two minutes away from knocking that raggedy ass lace front off.

I called Tosha on the way home...

"Hey girl, I'm sorry to bother you."

"Naw girl you good! I was just leaving a church function. What's going on?"

"Well I just wanted to tell you –"

"Hello? hello?" I said to myself.

Her phone must have died. I tried calling back but got no answer. When I got home, Derrick was still in the same spot he was when I left.

"Hey, is something going on with Tosha and Jazz? She called me and said she wanted to tell me something, then her phone went dead. It was super strange."

"She probably just needs someone to confine in. They are going through some marital problems right now."

"Aw poor Tosh.... I should have invited her tonight. I'll be sure to call her tomorrow. Right now, I need a hot shower and some sleep."

DERRICK

After Amber fell asleep, I texted Tosha.

"Why are you playing?"

She hit me back with three question mark symbols.

"Okay so you moving like that Tosha? Really?"

"I just wanted to get your attention."

"You got this woman thinking something is wrong with you. She said your phone went dead."

"Good that means it seemed real. I told you that I'm not going to just let you cut my line of dick credit off like that!"

"Here you go, I told you that we need to chill out…"

"I told you I wasn't ready to be done, now come over…"

"Girl I'm not coming over to my homeboy's house! I don't know what you on, but it can't be that bad between y'all to the point you feel the need to ask me to be that risky with you."

"Meet me at the gas station. If you don't, I promise I'm going to tell Jazz about us and call Amber back I'm for real this time!"

"Why are you doing this?"

"Because I want you in me… just come. I'll be there in 15 mins, it should take you 20 min to get there, I'll

be waiting on the side."

I put my phone down and got ready. I got there with time to spare; she was standing outside in the rain under the shield of the stores one-foot roof overhang. She ran over to the car rushing in.

"Hey Boo, I see you came!"

"I see you picked up some weight. What's going on girl?"

"Damn that's rude! If you must know I've been stressing, that's why, and I been needing some of this good quality dick!"

She grabbed me like she owned it.

"Damn you ready huh?"

"Apparently so are you."

"He just has a mind of his own, that's all that is, but question... how did you know that I would come?"

"Because pipes bust under pressure."

"Aw yeah, is that so?"

"Of course, I'll prove it to you."

She leaned over and started giving me head. As bad as I didn't want to be there, I was glad I came. I reclined my seat to further enjoy our worst behavior. About 4 mins into it someone knocked on the window, startling us both. We looked fearfully, like deer in headlights. I cracked the window.

"Hey G! You have some change? I'm trying to get a sandwich..."

"Nawh man, fall back!"

"Derrick! He was just hungry."

"Girl please! He probably has more money than both of us, you know most of them be scamming right?"

"Well he doesn't look like one of the scammers. He looks like he's really in need."

"Of course he did, just like the rest of them over there. That's what you do when you're trying to run game on someone. You look the part they really be taking turns begging for money, it's almost like a job. I'm not giving them shit!"

I drove to a dark alley and parked along the back fence of some abandoned two-story house.

"This is much better.", she said.

She tried to pick up where we left off, I leaned forward preventing her from reaching the target.

"Derrick chill! Move! You must think that I won't expose our secret the way you're playing with my emotions."

"Let's just talk, I always enjoy talking to you. It doesn't always have to be about sex, I thought we agreed to work things out at home?"

"You're starting to piss me off. Just give me what I want dang!"

"Tosha do you remember the first time we messed around? My brother Jazz told me I wasn't driving home and took my keys that night. He went to work and let my drunk ass sleep on his couch, not knowing his wife would rape his best friend."

"That's not what happened. You woke up in the middle of the night and came in my room remember? Also, it's not rape if it got hard and believe me, it was super hard."

"The point is, he has always looked out for me and this isn't right Tosha."

"Okay this is the last time; I promise just give it to me hard and heavy one last time."

She went back to sucking on my bone, extracting the first round of babies. I got my strength back up and bent her over the backseat rolling her panties down to her ankles. I went in, gripping the back of her neck, rocking in and out of her pussy like I was in my prime again. She gripped the grab bar on the ceiling.

"Ooo fuck yes!"

I felt the car rock with every hard stroke, forcing her

chest to confront the back seat. She yelled my name multiple times and reached her hand back to feel my nuts. Right before I came, she turned around to make her presence known. She swallowed my release until I pulled her well-oiled roots hella hard. We finished and I instantly felt nauseous. I was tired of doing this damage and deceiving the only true homeboy I had. I couldn't keep living this lie. I needed to be better and he deserved better from both of us. He put labor into being the man she needed and a good ass friend. Who was I to shit on his effort?

That weekend Jazz invited Ashley and I to hang out with him and the girls. We had nothing going on, plus Amber picked up an extra shift at work. I figured it was the least I could do, since I was the unknown source behind some of the madness happening in his life. We made it just in time, he was taking the meat off the grill.

"Hey Niece!"

He gave her a hug and we exchanged our routine greeting.

"What up boi! I appreciate y'all sliding through bro..."

"All day! You know what it is, and you know I'm not turning down the free food."

"I hear that, I'm not mad at it! There's plenty of it too.

What's going on with you, what's new?"

"That's what I came to see, you tell me... Are things getting any better between you and Tosha?"

"Not yet, her ass been sleeping a lot lately. She did say we need to talk, so I should know what her temperature is here soon."

He called the girls down.

"Y'all ready? Aye, we're about to go to the store. Do you and niece want to ride?"

"Yeah, we down."

We loaded up in the car and Jazz hyped the girls up.

"What all do y'all want? Y'all can have anything!"

They got overly excited yelling out all at once.

"Candy!"

"Chips!"

"Ice cream!"

"Ouuu pop!"

"Now y'all know y'all not getting pop! Y'all can have some juice."

I questioned his parenting skills.

"What's the difference bruh? They both have sugar. Get them some flavored water and they won't know the difference."

"Ugh, no uncle Derrick! We'll take juice Daddy!"

"See, my kids do juice, pop is bad for the skin and body. That's why you got all those bumps on your face boy!"

"Naw bruh! That's from a lack of punany!"

"That's what happens when you get married.", he laughed.

"You preaching to the choir big dog, hell you see the foolery I'm dealing with. I'm no dummy. I knew it had to be someone else. Think about this... how the hell are you tired every day and, on your period every two weeks? That don't add up at all bruh."

"How do you know she's not irregular or something? I wouldn't jump to the conclusion that she's cheating, maybe your overthinking it."

"I'm not jumping the gun. I just know... On top of that, I keep up with her period cycle. That pussy is good to go from the 1st to the 17th! It starts to drip between the 18th and 19th

and it locks up until the 28th. You know me well enough to know, that when I have a feeling about something, nine times out of ten, I'm right. She's been acting and moving real funny. It's someone else in the picture, trust me! We're starting to have simple stupid disagreements. One time she tried to tell me eggs don't have an expiration date!"

"Yeah, I know what you mean, it really be the little shit. A lack of sex will always have you wondering and questioning who's hitting it. I've had some of those moments myself when Amber would hold out, but you know me, I'm going to get it where I get it bro. I'll be honest, in the past I've created some unnecessary arguments a time or two over petty stuff, like why the hell do we have more forks than spoons type of shit, ya know?"

"We don't have more forks than spoons uncle Derrick" someone small chimed in.

"Stay out of grown folks' conversations Jayla, I told y'all about that!"

"Yeah and why y'all back there asking for the whole store? Y'all must be rich or something huh...?"

"No uncle Derrick y'all are!"

"Nia, you must be talking about your mama and daddy because uncle Derrick is broke! Just like your daddy's jump shot."

"Man what?! Yeah okay, my jumper on point, you could never stop it!"

"The lies you tell..."

"Man please, anytime you're ready, it's a court down the street from the house. I'm available from 10AM to

6PM, Monday through Friday, and flexible on the weekends."

"You talking all that noise and know you don't want no smoke."

"Listen man, we are going to pick this conversation up when I get back, see if your willing to put that money where that mouth is."

Don't Leave Me...

I stayed in the car with the girls, I felt eyes watching me. I turned around and Jayla was staring directly at me. I knew that she knew it was me in the room that night, I gave her the uncomfortable *you better not say shit face* and remained silent. I went back to scrolling through my phone. Suddenly, Nia screamed.

"Daddy!"

I looked up out the window and saw Jazz tussling with some heavy nigga. I jumped out running over, getting my hands involved. Jazz freed up, throwing combos. We dropped his ass right outside the door of the store.

"What the Fuck! You bitch niggas got the wrong one!", His homeboy yelled.

173

Shots rang out!

We rushed back to the car. I got in the driver seat because I knew Jazz slow ass wouldn't beat me there.

"Hurry up go, go!"

I sped off, leaving tire marks behind.

"Oh shit!"

"Daddy, what happened?" Jayla asked afraid.

"Just some nonsense boo, I'm sorry y'all had to see that." he said warmly.

"Okay now, grown man status.... what the hell really happened back there?" I asked once we were miles away from the store.

"His big ass was coming out as I was going in and he deliberately bumped into me like I was less of a man or something! So, I helmed him up!"

"Looked like you were getting helmed from this angle... I'm just saying."

"Yeah right, I tell you all the time -- anything with weight can fall!"

"Yeah because I did most of the damage, yo ass was wrestling with him."

"Yea okay, I gave him that work, and you came and finished him off, but I got him!" "Either way we're not young no more, I can't be doing all this extra with you. It was fun tho, brings back memories!"

"We were scared", Nia said.

"Nia it's okay to be scared niece. Ash what about you boo? You ok?"

"I think she's sleeping uncle Derrick."

Nia pulled her finger to try and wake her up, then shook her little belly. I looked in the rear-view mirror to see Nia's eyes enlarge as she pulled back her hand. Her fingers were covered in blood.

"Nia what's tha --."

Jazz yelled, "Pull over D, pull over!"

Jazz climbed over the seat to get to Ashley.

"No, no, no, no, no..." was all I could say.

Jazz took his shirt off applying pressure to the wound.

"It's gon be okay niece, I got you! Hold on baby. We'll get to a hospital! Quick hurry D!"

I rushed knowing only one thing – my baby was shot. I nearly crashed into the emergency entrance of the hospital. Jazz exited the car with Ashley before I could put it in park. I followed in a state of panic with his girls behind me crying. They took her to a restricted area, and we couldn't do anything but pace in the waiting room helplessly. I couldn't believe what was happening. I contacted Amber and she wasted no time getting to us. She was confused about the whole incident and trying to piece it together.

"So y'all were coming - I mean where did this? Oh my God! Jesus, this can't be real! Okay, okay... Oh Lord have mercy on us! When did y'all notice!?"

"I -- we just, it all happened so fast...", I trailed almost out of my mind.

Jazz took over.

"Sis, we were at the gas station getting snacks and drinks for the girls. Shit got messy and some dude started shooting. We got out of there quickly but didn't think anything of it until we came to notice that she wasn't interacting. We got here as soon as we could."

The doctor came out with a disturbing look on her face, we all braced ourselves, fearing the worst.

"Hi, I'm Doctor Boyle. I want you to know that we have her stable but..." she paused.

"She lost a lot of blood. The bullet entered her left side, piercing a vital organ. Ultimately, causing respiratory failure."

"Okay we just, what are you saying because we need a clear understanding. None of this makes sense, I don't understand what any of this means.", Amber said.

"She is battling respiratory failure, hypercapnia to be

specific, which is a rise in her arterial oxygen levels. To say the least, her lungs could collapse. Meaning, unfortunately, the chance of her surviving is very unlikely, but I assure you, we are still doing everything in our power. We will continue to do all that we can to make sure she's as comfortable as she can be. You guys will be able to see her shortly."

We were all at a loss for words.

Amber cried on my shoulder and began hitting me several times.

"How could you let this happen to our baby!?"

The guilt piled up as she released from me to stroll down the hall trying to pull herself together. They finally gave us clearance to see her, we weren't strong enough to visit all at once. Amber went in first.

I sat with my hands over my head wondering where I went wrong, *Why her? Why me? why us?*...after a while I walked in to see Ashley's small body hooked up to machines keeping her alive. Seeing her that way was the hardest thing ever. I sat in the chair beside the bed with my head hanging over her body, not wanting to accept that this was reality.

"Hey baby, you are everything to me" I began. "You are the reason my heart beats. I'm so sorry. You are the last person who deserves this, and I'm scared to live without you."

It was hard to fight back the tears that were making their way uncontrollably out of the corners of my eyes. I rested my head on her, begging her to keep fighting.

"Please don't give up, don't leave me baby! You can't leave me; I need you here!"

Humble

It was 7:46 pm when they pronounced her dead.

Ashley's death was unreal and so sudden. We couldn't afford to bury her, so we decided to have her cremated. Not what we would have liked for our baby, but it was all that we could afford under the circumstances. Our world had been officially rocked. We were caught off guard and beginning to self-destruct. Never in a lifetime did we imagine that we would be forced to meet a curse so cruel.

Months passed and we were still feeling the aftershock of losing our child. It was an emotional earthquake. I placed blame on myself, and I hated Jazz with every fiber of my body. I couldn't eat and didn't eat. No matter how many times I cried in the flat space of this car, where I came to reside after Amber and I separated, the pain never seemed to cease. It was an unwanted host. I couldn't sleep, my mind replayed the scary movie over and over. I lost my heart and the one person that could bring normalcy ignored my texts and forwarded all my calls.

I was empty inside and buried to my lowest point. It became clear to me that I had no more options because there was no solution. The rain beat radically against all the windows, drowning my car, it seemed. I held the gun to my temple unsteadily, just then a gospel artist, whose song spoke of hills and valleys, played in the heart of the quiet storm, which normally consist of love making music on the radio. It was as if the source that I rejected so many times saw me despair. Maybe I was delusional, but I tried everything else and I was desperate enough to do anything to numb the pain. Following the voice that deferred death that night, I attended church service that following Sunday. I visually searched the crowed for Amber with no luck of seeing her in attendance. I stood in the far front staring in space at the lighting that ignited character to the pulpit. Vocals of the guest singer caught me off guard, her voice was flawless and pure, like it came with a warranty from heaven. For the first time, church felt like a place I belonged.

In the middle of her song she said something that stood out to me.

"There's a sound that God adores... it's called worship. Can we put that in the atmosphere right now? Can we release a sound of surrender in this place? Occasionally GOD will break you into position. Whew! Thank you Jesus!"

I submitted all that I had, stretching my arms and hands out far and wide, to feel the chains of the devil's trap break. I found myself chanting in defeat...

"Forgive me! You can have me! I quit; you win!"

I failed to hold back my tears. I cried like a baby and even harder when I felt the arms of another man embrace me like the Father I always needed. It took me a while to pull myself together. He never let go.

Pastor begin to pray over me.

"Father you move mountains, move this mountain of pain and heartache Lord! Restore joy in his spiritual room, make his heart available to receive healing Father! Lord we know to be absent from this world is to be present in yours. Let the Ross family and all who have been effected by this devastating loss of a beautiful spirit, find comfort in knowing that you still live!"

He prayed to the higher power real strong, like he meant it. The worship team ushered in another song. I joined the church in singing, *"Give me you, everything else could wait."* ... and it would.

I made it through church feeling unselfish. I knew my baby's destiny was fulfilled and I explored the confidence of knowing she now resided in the heavens. Pastor pulled me aside after service.

"How are you holding up Derrick?"

"Barely, I've been having a real difficult time accepting everything."

"Sometimes the devil's strategy is to make us feel defeated to withdraw faith and the only way to do that, is to attack when we are weak."

"I'm in a dark place. Ashley is gone and Amber left me. I tried everything to get her back, but I feel alone, my head is in a cloudy place."

"It's not over."

"No, Pastor, I'm pretty sure it's over. She wants nothing to do with me."

"That may be true at this moment. You guys have entered a hard place right now and she is grieving, just like you. This is the part where no one can offer words of relief, and no one can guarantee brighter days will come.

This is the part where you trust God enough to say, I don't know the plan, and the hurt seems like more than I can stand, but I'm glad you have chosen to use me for your will. No matter the situation, even when it doesn't feel good, when it feels like hell is all around me, I'll worship. It's not going to be an easy road, but the bible says, *"Whoever belongs to God, hears what God says.* Amber is of God, her faith has soul, if you know what I mean.",

We kind of chuckled

"Yeah, I see what you're saying."

"She'll hear God, I'm certain. Tell you what? My wife and I will try reaching out to her to see if she's interested in sitting down with us, but without force of course. It must be on her terms, when she's ready she'll come. For now, I want you to get into the word, pray, and keep your thoughts and spirits up lifted. The devil knows when to attack and you must be ready to reject all his invitations to every depression party that he cast your way."

"Yes Sir, most definitely."

"I'm serious Derrick, were both men. We can be stubborn, and there is nothing wrong with hurting. The same way there is nothing wrong with releasing our pain into the universe, without the tough act. God sees his child, you remember that."

We hugged it out, which was probably the most mature thing I've ever done as a man. Kim stood alone in the walkway, waiting for me to come out. She hugged me in an idle, like she was hurting for me.

"I'm so sorry for your loss Derrick, how are you doing?"

"I'm not sure but I'll make it. There's nothing that God can't heal, right?"

As a tear ran down her cheek, she apologized.

"I'm sorry, you're going to make me cry. I just get emotional thinking about everything. I have no words; I hate that this is happening to you boo. How's your wife dealing with everything?"

"I couldn't tell you. I haven't seen or spoke to her in months."

"Wow. I know this is hard for you both. I'm free if you want to come over tonight, you really shouldn't be unaccompanied during a time like this."

"Thank you but I'll pass. I have a lot going on, just trying to figure out who I am."

"You're a good man who's hurting and needs attention. Don't try to come out of this alone. I'm here for you and my offer always stands. Call me if you need anything, and I do mean anything."

She hugged me once again kissing me respectfully on the cheek.

Night came and Jazz had the nerve to call my phone back to back. As many times as I ignored him, it didn't do any good with the devil stalking close behind, poisoning my mental with guilt and shame unapologetically. I tried to dismiss the feeling by forcing myself to sleep, but even that birthed intense consequences, causing me to wake in the mid hour. My dreams served as an enemy that I couldn't hide from; my mind was a troubled prisoner. My problem felt like it had problems. On top of the back pain that this make ship bed offered, it was all bad with no relief in sight. I thought if I spoke aloud it would withdraw this demon harassing me.

"God, I know I'm new at this whole talking to you thing. I know I'm not a perfect model of your will. I'm lost but I'm here. I'm committed to you. Please spare me of this hurt. Haven't I suffered enough? You have taken everything good from me. What more is there to give? I have nothing. I get it. I just want my wife back; I promise to be a better man. I promise to trust you God. I trust you now and I will no longer be the same person if you just restore my marriage. Bring my wife back to me, that's all. I'm begging you."

185

A few days later I was at work trying to make it through my day, and Issac said something that got me to thinking maybe God didn't hear my prayers. I felt alone and was deeply saddened by the promise of Amber coming around. That promise started to seem farfetched and it was hard not talking to her for so long. Issac tried to lighten the moment by being his usual self, but it didn't matter, I couldn't connect with his underdeveloped jokes. I had far too much going on.

He said something that I didn't even think of, maybe the smartest thing he has ever said.

"Dude you know you can crash in any of these vacant units, right? I do it all the time. When Marissa gets to talking her major shit. I bring my ass right over here."

"Man, I didn't even think about that. I could use a decent place to lay at night, I be uncomfortable as hell trying to stretch out in the back of the car."

"I bet. You're better than me bruh. I mean you're already going through hell, don't suffer more than you need to homie. This is one of the benefits to working maintenance at a community property. I call it the *bonus we never get;* you better use these resources."

"I think you're on to something, that sort of makes sense. I'm sho going to use it, starting tonight. It does feel like they owe us something."

"You damn right they do!"

THERE IS BEAUTY IN BROKENNESS

I took advantage of the temporary shelter for a couple

of weeks. One night I was looking out of the window and

saw Andrea who lived in the complex across the way. She

was looking like a whole snack in her bonnet and house

shoes. I almost started to relapse to the old me and

question God's authority over my life, as an excuse to

revert. I had yet to receive confirmation on my outpour. It

had been so long since I touched a woman. I continued to

watch then decided to be strong and not allow the devil to

exercise in my mind. Although it smelled like fried

chicken in this unit, I felt blessed. Maybe I was close to

doing something right because that next morning I received a text that felt like hope.

"Good morning! There is nothing too hard for God. We are planning to meet this Saturday at noon with your wife, please be available. I look forward to seeing you.

First Lady Victoria 😊 "

The smiley face after her name resembled the face I made after reading her message. I was a kid filled with excitement. I was in disbelief and couldn't believe I was going to see my wife. The closer the day came, the more mixed my emotions got. I became sad, scared, and nervous all in one sitting. I wasn't sure how this would play out. I didn't know if she would accept the man I was becoming or at least trying to be. It was like the first day of school. I got my clothes together and even wrote my feelings down. I wanted to be prepared and make sure she knew I was willing to fight for her.

Saturday came and the outcome of us embracing each other and sharing the same space was a far reach. In fact, our meeting was nothing like I thought it would be. She was there but quiet, she looked more beautiful than ever, she mostly listened with very little input.

Pastor got straight to the point.

"Amber do you think the passing of Ashley caused strain on your marriage?"

"I think this marriage was a mistake. I think I stayed unhappy for too long and I think I wasted a lot of time with a man who didn't know how to love."

"Baby I do know how to love.... I'm sorry I couldn't see how immature I was as a man. I just want you now."

"It's too late for that Derrick, were done..."

"Don't say that babe, you don't mean it. I'm hurting too. You're not alone in this."

"Now you want to be all strategic and caring. You weren't thinking of me when you were fucking my cousin. I'm sorry -- excuse me Pastor and First Lady -- screwing my cousin."

"What, what are you talking about? I've never touched Jessica!"

"Oh, how do you know I'm talking about Jessica?"

"Amber, she tried it. But I promise you I shut that mess down."

"Yeah sure you did, that's why you never told me about it!"

"I didn't tell you because it was nothing!"

"Nothing to who Derrick!? Everything is nothing to you! Clearly, I'm nothing to you as well. Even if you didn't sleep with Jessica, I'm sure something happened. Just like the something that often happens when you leave in the middle of the night. What, you think I don't know about your chat sites?"

"I did not leave in the middle of the nights Amber. It was late at times but never the middle of the night, you're over exaggerating now!" I lied, getting nervous.

"Is that your defense?"

Pastor Herman intervened, "I think we need to step back and reevaluate the direction we're going in. Derrick do you truly love your wife?"

"Yes, I do. I really do."

"You don't love me! Not only did u lose our daughter but..."

Pastor interrupted her before she could finish,

"Wait a minute Amber, let's all just take a moment. I know your hurting and sometimes hurt can lead to unfair statements, but this is not one sided. You both feel it, you both have endured a painful experience. The only way to get through this, is by understanding each other."

"What's there to understand? We have unnecessary arguments, he's a cheater, a liar, and I honestly don't see any reason for us to pursue a marriage built on betrayal. We no longer share a bond because our daughter is gone.

She is dead and not coming back. Question.... while we're here... Did you really expect me to believe you were out with Jazz all those late nights? I knew every time you stuttered; you're lying. I'm not the dummy you played me for!"

"Amber don't act like you're innocent. What about that bruise you had on your behind the day after Valentine's Day?"

"Oh, you mean the time I fell down the stairs because my so-called husband couldn't put salt on the ice outside?... But sure Derrick, try your best to turn it around on me! Believe what you want to believe because we're done! I mean it this time!"

"Do you guys know that God created marriage to be a good thing? He never said it was going to be an easy thing, that's why he tells us to cover one another. When was the last time you actually prayed for one another?"

"Pastor I've been praying for her almost daily here lately."

Amber chuckled.

"Yeah right, there's another one of your lies."

Pastor and First Lady looked at each other like they had a trick up their sleeve, then First Lady Victoria came up with an idea.

"This is a very sensitive time and we know that sometimes situations of this caliber can bring out the worst in two ppl who are trying to make it work but suffering in a painful experience. It's not easy but I believe God is a super-natural healer. He creates and never divides. How about we change it up a bit? Sometimes we must vent separately to heal jointly. Tell you what Amber, why don't you and I spend some time together? I think it would be therapeutic for you to have an open line to clear out your storage box and maybe we can try this again in a few weeks. How does that sound?"

"Umm, I guess it couldn't hurt but I'm sure it won't change my mind."

"Good, because I'm not here to persuade you or change your decision. I just want to help you with the healing aspect for now and if we can revisit this afterwards than we will."

Pastor said, "That sounds good to me. Derrick let's allow God to work. I want you to continue leaning on your faith and faithfully embracing the word. If its ok, I'll be in touch."

As we prepared to depart First Lady gave me a long inviting hug. As we separated, she grabbed both of my hands and said, "Continue your fight. You deserve all that God has for you and it will be okay", with a giant smile and a wink of assurance.

AMBER

I kept up my end of the deal and scheduled a time to meet with First Lady at the church, in the small east corner meeting room that Thursday night. We sat and talked about faith, who I am, and how I was coping with the loss of Ashley for the longest. Then the conversation dove deeper, with her asking multiple questions that I wasn't totally comfortable with, but I knew I had to be open minded since she was kind enough to reach out. I considered it all a part of my healing process.

TRYING PLACES

It was time for me to stop hiding and holding back, I had nothing more to lose, it was time for me to get it all out.

"So, if I may ask Amber, how is your married sex life? And the reason I say married, is because sex seems to change after marriage and we women sometimes must adapt. It's not always the same once a man gets comfortable."

"Sometimes I just lay there wide awake after sex. I mean don't get me wrong, it's good, but it's not what it used to be. I admit, after he's sleep, I have to take my toy and finish what he started."

First Lady looked harder at me than she ever had. I

197

couldn't tell if I was being judged or if she was deep in thought.

"Are you aware that sex is eighty percent mental and twenty percent sexual? If a man does not have your mind, you'll never be satisfied. It doesn't matter how much history you have, how married you are, or how in love you are. If he does not stimulate your mind first, your body will not follow. Then there's the technique aspect, what and how you like it may be different, possibly changing with age. So how do you like it? And how do you do it?"

Not quite understanding. I asked,

"What do you mean?... like how can I do something like that?"

"No, when you're playing with yourself, how do you rub your toy against your private area?" she said.

I looked down with embarrassment and took a sip of wine. She scooted closer and placed her hand on my thigh, verbally assuring me it's ok to let her in.

I mumbled the words right out of my mouth, "In a circular motion."

"Soft like, or kinda aggressive, like this?"

Dipping her hands in between my sundress, demonstrating with the tip of her four fingers pressed firmly against my clit, she started rubbing.

"Is it like this?"

Nervous, but complying, I nodded. My neck balanced in a slow lean to the side licking my lips.

"Ummm, maybe slightly softer." I managed.

She eased up, rubbing less aggressively, using her other hand to remove my drink, placing it on the table in front of us.

"I don't know if ..."

"Shhhh" the First Lady began.

She had control moving her hand closer to my vagina. My eyes closed and I could feel my wetness seeping. I blatantly interrupted wiggling away.

"I'm sorry, I should go."

I grabbed my purse and got out of there. I sat in the car for some time with my head down over the steering wheel, trying to make sense of everything. I wasn't close to having it together, but I couldn't sit there forever. I was poised enough to drive away. I felt horrible and even worse... I still felt horny from her bold actions. I pulled out my small bullet from the armrest and took an unusual risk. A continuous vibration spoiled the top half of my womanhood as I cruised down I-75 highway. The buzzing noise substituted the background music. I felt her energy invading me still, it wasn't until another driver honked at me for swerving in their lane, that I realized just how I absorbed her actions.

That evening, I raised the windows in the bathroom to watch the night cover the sky like a blanket. I submerged my body in a small pool of steaming hot water smothered with a cloud of foam. No music was necessary. Her touch alone was rhythmic, jogging through my mind.

Time quickly escaped from me. It was 3am and I laid in bed restless, tossing, and turning, finally positioning myself to face the wall. I started scrolling through social media videos. I came across an old F.P.C.O.C broadcast sermon of Pastor preaching about how God will disable you so that you may enable him, he said…

"Don't ask God for something that you're not willing to struggle for."

That struck a chord with me. All this time, I had been praying for God to change my husband for the better and maybe this was his way of doing that. Although I never thought that it would come with this level of pain and sacrifice. Regardless, I never saw Derrick so serious and determined. I had asked God for something and it seemed as if he responded. I was still trying to wrap my head around the give and take concept, and thought I'd never understand it, but I knew I was starting to miss him.

Without family, our home felt cold and lonely. I got sad thinking about it.

I started to type out a text to him then erased it trying to be strong. I soon thought about how childish I was acting. I wanted my husband, so I made the call letting it ring one and a half times before quickly hanging up. A millisecond had barely gone by before he called back. I let the phone ring until it went silent, his persistence had me feeling loved, he called back to back. I finally answered putting on a front, clearing my throat as if I were asleep.

"Hello?"

"Hey um, hello, good morning, you called?"

"No not that I know of."

"Oh well I thought -- I mean, I had a missed call from you, is everything alright?"

"Yeah I'm fine must have been by mistake."

"Oh, I see. I'm sorry to bother you. I'll let you get back to sleep."

Right before he hung up, I called out to him.

"Hey Derrick!"

"Yes?"

"Are you okay?"

"I miss her, and you like crazy, but other than that I'm maintaining. Just drowning my head in the word, you know, trying my best to be obedient."

"Where are you staying?"

"Most of the time in my car, but lately, I've been crashing at work."

"Why? You know... never mind. Can you please come home?" I said, the words clinging to the back of my throat.

"You sure?! I mean you don't have to feel sorry ..."

"Derrick, please just come home. I just want you here."

"Are you serious?"

"Yes, Derrick. Just come home."

He heard my cry and came home, letting himself in. He climbed in bed cuddling me. I laid in his arms and cried my heart out. We both called into work the next day, choosing to vent over brunch instead of laboring the day away mindlessly. He held my hand and opened every door; it was like the beginning of a new relationship. I felt protected. For months, this went on and though we weren't active in church, his outlook changed.

He prayed constantly even when I didn't, he was becoming the man I always wanted, the man I asked God for. However, I failed to match his energy.

I was still hurting, and still in a very dark state of mind with no closure in sight. I visited Ashley's burial site daily. Somedays I stayed until the sun set, I truly missed my baby and it was hard to let her be.

THE BEGINNING AND THE END

 Three months had gone by since that awkward moment First Lady and I created. Since then I manage to avoid church like the plague, so of course I found it random on top of weird that she would contact me to see if I wanted to talk. Especially since our last encounter went all the way left. I was super iffy but also curious to see what she had to say. After receiving a combination of texts from her, I figured, -- *"hell why not go see what it is she has to say"* --. I had been depressed looking at these four walls and everything had been so abnormal for me. I believed I probably did need to talk to someone.

"Thank you for coming Amber! I hope I'm not interrupting anything. I haven't been seeing you at church and I've been really concerned about you. Something in my spirit just wanted to make sure you were okay. I know this journey isn't easy nor will I sit here and pretend that I know what it's like to lose a child, because I don't -- hell Lewis and I can't even have kids.", she divulged.

"But regardless, I do know that losing a loved one in general is hard. I can only imagine your situation and the stress, that's why I called you over."

"It's okay First Lady, I didn't have any plans, I was home alone actually. Ever since Derrick and I decided to work it out, he has been occupying his time with extra work. I guess I can't blame him for wanting to keep busy. I admit I still have my moments; this has been the hardest 7 months in my life. I miss her smile, her cry, her kisses...but I've been managing."

"I'm sure it has been long, tough, and trying for the both of you. We all cope differently honey. Just continue to support his healing process. My question to you is, what's your way of healing?"

"One day at a time I guess, not sure that I have one. I just wake up and try not to cry, but I do, every day I do."

"You know what? Come here, I want to show you

something."

She helped me up and guided me through the beautiful, well lit, open floor plan of her high vaulted ceiling home. We walked into the room where her bed stood elevated. She took me into the closet. Her clothes literally had their own damn room, her storage had storage! She started pulling clothes down that still had tags on them.

"Here, try these on. I never got a chance to wear them and they kind of just hang here abandoned."

"No, I couldn't. This is way too expensive to play in or have on. Do you see the price on these?" My eyes opened wide, "this is the amount of my mortgage!" I screamed.

"I'm sorry, I can't First Lady."

"Amber, I know what it costs sweetie, I bought it. And stop calling me that! You can call me Victoria. Now would you stop acting all stuck up and try the dang dress on! Please? I'm not taking no for an answer, so we can stand here and go back and forth all day, but rejection is not an option." she hinted.

I took a deep breath, "Okay, okay, where do you want me to try them on?"

"Right here, it's just us here, don't be shy. We're both

women. We got the same woman parts, nothing I haven't seen honey trust me, go ahead."

As strange as it felt, I just went with it. She watched closely as I unfastened my pants. It was like she undressed me faster than I could pull them down. I was just pleased with the fact that I had on matching panties and bra, which spared me the embarrassment. She was a bit intimidating, but something in me felt the need to impress her. Maybe it was the fact that she was our First Lady, I guess.

She slid the black Gianvito dress over my head. I put my arms through it and pulled it past the stretch marks on the sides of my stomach. It was a snug fit. Once I had it on, she adjusted it with her hands in certain areas, pinching it here and there before turning me to face her giant mirror. I felt pretty for the first time in a long time. She pulled my hair back talking in a soothing way right by my earlobe. It was as if she already knew it was my spot.

"See, this fits you perfectly! You look amazing! Hell, I don't think you could have filled this any better. You have a gorgeous body Amber." She said serenading me. I hadn't been complimented in forever. I was already emotional, so to hear something positive brought me to tears.

"Aw don't cry love…"

She took her finger and wiped the standing tear from my face, then unexpectedly she introduced her lips to my neck, kissing slow and steady, temporarily paralyzing my body. My head started to lean in acceptance. It seemed like a to-be-continued episode of our last session

"I can't, we shouldn't be..." I began.

"Shhhh. Just relax honey."

"But we ..."

She must have rehearsed. She rapidly responded in a soft-spoken voice, before I could say anything to reroute the crash course.

"It's okay, we're not hurting anyone sweetheart. Rejection isn't an option remember, live in the moment, we're already here."

She was right. I felt the wetness all around my inner thighs. My mother would always say-- *"The greatest feeling in the heart, is being two centimeters away from kissing the lips of someone you know damn well you have no business fooling with"* -- It only took a few seconds of me trying to negotiate myself out of this wet tantric and very karmic dream, before a part of me heard the devil say, *"Fuck it!"*. I felt certain that I was too deep to pull away. I turned around and leaned forward to kiss her full filled lips. A second tear rolled down my face, right into our exchange. She ran her hands underneath my dress palming my soft ass and kissing me like we had chemistry. Her transition was flawless. I was slow to notice her hands had repositioned, sliding in the creative space underneath my selfish lace panties. Her fourplay delivery was patient and consistent. I hadn't felt this kind of joy in some time. Her fingers became one with my clit, touching me slower than a 90's r&b song. I was clearly hypnotized, watching her remove her now creamy fingers from the warm pocket in between my wide thighs, only to place them inside her juicy mouth. We sheltered our half naked bodies on the floor of her beautiful closet, as if the outside world no longer existed. She sucked the wetness off the center of my under garment, while moving them to the side with her teeth. She reached in a shoe box and pulled out a large vibrating dildo, placing it against the surface of my pussy It pulsated. My body reacted without restriction, almost instantly forming a river with current inside my ravine well. I took the lead grabbing her hand with the rubber joystick, pushing it inside me. My pussy clamped tighter with every small but intentional vibration. She wrapped her arms underneath my legs, drowning my clit in the warmth of her mouth. My eyes rolled back.

"Uhhh God! Yes oouuu, no, no -- wait -- hold on! hold

on!"

I had to force her to quit. Her tongue was too experienced for me. I stopped us both before I came all over her face.

"What's wrong honey?"

"Nothing, I… I'm sorry, I didn't want to make a mess on you. I was close..."

"Well I wish you did! I'm not down here to stay dry I want you to release."

"I'm sorry, I just…"

"It's okay hun, come here."

She started sucking on my thick nipples while rubbing my clit counterclockwise. She made sure I was good and wet then intertwined her legs with mine in a pretzel like position, ready to scissor. Our warm oceans met in the middle. My heart raced uncontrollably. Her bare pussy grinded against mine with pleasure.

"Oh my goodness, you feel so good Amber! Ooouu, you're so wet babe."

We bumped long and hard, then slow and harder. She started to squirt and so did I.

"Oohhh fuck! I like the way you fuck me! Mmmhhh harder, oh ou fuuucck me please, I'm about to cum!"

"Ouu! Yea baby? Me too! Yes, yes, yes shit yes!"

Our forces collided as we climaxed sending our bodies into small convulsions. We rained on each other for about 15 seconds or more. In the aftermath, we just laid there connected to each other in a loop of wetness and ecstasy. Her body still throbbing against mine.

"You okay?"

"I'm not sure yet, but that was amazing. I don't even - - how? Where did you learn that? Wow!"

"Are you serious? Is this your first encounter with a woman?" she asked.

"For the most part, I've never done anything this extensive with a woman. I mean, I've kissed a woman, well I guess at that time we were just girls experimenting in the bathroom in elementary. So no, to answer you. Not really. Nothing at all like this. I've never really been gay gay."

"Gay? I believe all women are a little bi curious. I refuse to believe women can be gay though. All fetuses are initially female at first."

"Okay you lost me..."

"Okay, think about it like this, it's been proven scientifically that we're all conceived as females first. So, there is no way we can even remotely be considered gay."

I cracked up laughing. I was in total disbelief.

"You mean to tell me...God referred to us as man? How? I mean what about the passage where Eve ate the apple from the tree in the garden?"

"Great point to my suggestion actually, I know it sounds a bit confusing but look -- Eve was first to eat the apple, right? That tells it all. We are the tree honey, and our vaginas are the apples! God also gave man the woman as a helper. He knew man alone couldn't keep a woman satisfied. The kicker is understanding what the message is really suggesting. Now of course the disciples couldn't be direct and say, *"And woman ate the pussy of woman, as it was plentiful and of wisdom."* No, that would have been too direct. So, they said, *"She took some and ate it."* Then it said, *"She gave some to her husband who was with her."* Now understand, that had her husband not been there, he wouldn't have got the opportunity to taste it at all. We have the power to share, not them."

"Wow! That's definitely a different way of thinking and hard to digest. I really wouldn't expect you of all people to, never mind."

"--- No, no don't do that, speak your mind! What because I'm married to the leader of a church? I'm me first, and that's what's most difficult. Fronting for a congregation on Sunday morning, that only sees me as this super perfect wife of the Pastor. Don't get me wrong, I love the Lord -- but I struggle in areas just like the rest of you all."

"I'm sorry I didn't mean it like..."

"Like what?" She climbed over me and lingered.

"I'm just playing beautiful." She said leaning in to kiss me.

"I'm fully aware that I'm being an accomplice in these wrongful acts, but I couldn't resist. It felt good, good like that joyful moment your heart inherits when you vibe with someone you just met."

We smiled and cuddled like we were trying to produce a future together. She kissed the crease of my mouth again.

"You like that?"

"Well if you want my verbal truth. I would be lying if..."

I was cut short by the voice of Pastor Herman.

"Hey Babe! Wifey! Where are you love?"

My stomach dropped, both of our eyes locked in. She tried not to panic but it was clear that she was entering stage two of *"oh shit!"*. For the first time in my life, I felt like the white girl who didn't belong. She covered my mouth, giving me the universal sign to be quiet. I felt his heavy feet edge closer with every step, matching my heartbeat. She hopped up faster than we nutted, grabbing her robe off the hook. I was trapped and nervously sweating, regretting the dumb ass decision I made to fucking come here. Suddenly the door creaked open.

"What in the Devil's hell!!…"

To be continued…

Enjoyed this book?

Leave it a review and share it with a friend.

www.readsis.com